Out-Sniffed

Susan J. Kroupa

Published by Laurel Fork Press
Laurel Fork, Virginia
www.laurelforkpress.com

Photo and Cover Credits:
Labradoodle © 2012 by Susan J. Kroupa
3D Teddy Bear © Sebastian Kaulitzki | Dreamstime.com
No Bed Bugs © Morgan Oliver | Dreamstime.com
Brown & Black Bed Bug © Morgan Oliver | Dreamstime.com
Mobile Phone Case © Singkamic | Dreamstime.com
Cover Design © 2012 by Susan J. Kroupa
Book Design by Marny K. Parkin

In memory of my mother, Hazel Bigelow Stockwell.

From my earliest childhood until her death
at the much-too-young age of eighty-nine,
she modeled a life filled with courage and
an ever-eager passion for learning,
and she taught me, as well, to love dogs.

Contents

Chapter 1

Career Day

Bed bugs. Disgusting, right?

At least I know they are to humans. I've eaten a bed bug or two in my day and can't say they taste any worse than flies, which really aren't bad. But humans detest them because bed bugs live off human blood. And Molly says their bites itch as badly as flea bites itch dogs, which, I can tell you, is a lot. So I don't blame them for the detesting part.

The good thing about bed bugs is that the boss—that's Molly's father—and I have a job finding them. I do the actual finding, of course. The boss gets the jobs and drives us to the places so I can search. When I find them, I get paid in treats, which makes it all worthwhile. And since the job also includes Molly, I have what the boss calls a win-win situation. So I don't hate bed bugs. To me, they're just part of a day's work.

Which is why I'm at Molly's school with the boss. It's Career Day. All the parents come and tell the kids about their jobs, and since the boss can't do his work without me, I get to come too.

Molly practically glows with excitement. She's talked about little else for days.

"No one else gets to bring a dog," she says. "Everyone's going to want to pet Doodle."

And she's right. Even though I'm wearing my vest that says "Working. Please Don't Pet Me," all her classmates crowd around trying to touch me. Molly stands beside me radiating pride. But also some anxiety, which puzzles me. She keeps checking her watch and looking at the door as if she's expecting someone.

"His coat feels funny," says a boy who smells like hotdogs and sweat.

"He's a labradoodle," Molly tells him, explaining that I have a poodle rather than a Labrador retriever coat. "They were bred so their coats don't shed and they're hypoallergenic."

"I'm allergic to peanuts," a wispy girl with big glasses says softly. She darts a hand at the top of my head, touching me lightly, then jerking her hand back as if she's afraid I might snap it off. If she knew anything about dogs she could tell there's no chance of that. I mean, read my body language. And while her flying hands make me a little nervous, not to mention I don't really like having my head patted, being polite in public is part of the job. At least that's what my first trainer used to say.

"That makes him easy to take care of," the hot dog boy says.

"Not hardly," the boss says with some feeling. He rubs his beard in the way he does when he's a little nervous, adding that instead of hair, I shed the entire outside environment onto the house floors. He calls me Velcro-Boy. I don't understand what he means, but the kids aren't listening anyway.

"We have to get him groomed every few months," Molly says. "It can be expensive." But she strokes my back, her eyes soft with affection.

"Okay, everyone in their seats," Molly's teacher says in a deep, resonant voice. She's wearing earrings, big shiny loopy ones. Part of my service dog training involved retrieving earrings and other jewelry. Our trainers never gave us treats if we swallowed them. Just sayin'.

The teacher has skin the color of chocolate—something the boss never gives me—like Tanya Franklin, Molly's best friend, and she's almost as tall and lean as Tanya's brothers. Her hair curls close to her head, like mine just after a trip to the groomer.

"Hello. I'm Ms. Mandisa," the teacher says. "I'd like to welcome you all to Tri-State Science Academy. We're delighted to have you here. If everyone will take a seat—parents, we've set up extra chairs along the wall—we'll begin."

After a worried glance at her wrist and at the classroom door, Molly leads me to her desk, while the boss stands next to Mrs. Franklin, who's setting up a camera on a tripod over in the back corner of the room. Hey, Tanya's desk is right by Molly's. How great is that?

Tanya reaches over and scratches under my chin, something I happen to like very much. I've been friends with Tanya—with the whole Franklin family, in fact—ever since the time I sort of got lost and ended up in her yard.

We sit—well, actually, I lie down—for a long time while different parents talk to the class. I doze off. Then I hear the teacher say "Josh Hunter of Hunter Bed Bug Detection" and I sit up just as Molly hands the leash to the boss. He leads me up front.

"Ever seen a bed bug?" he asks. A few kids raise their hands. "Oh, I'm sorry to hear that. I hope you didn't find them in your bed!" The kids laugh and roll their eyes. He takes out a couple of vials with live bed bugs. "Pass these around while I tell you a little about the job."

The vials make their way through the classroom accompanied by sounds of eewww and yuck. As I said, to humans, disgusting.

"Scent detection dogs are also called sniffer dogs," the boss says. "Do you know why that is?"

The head-patting girl raises a hand. "Because they use their nose?"

"Exactly. A dog's sense of smell is up to 100 times more sensitive than a human's. We have about 5 million olfactory sensory cells—those are the cells to help us interpret what we smell. Some breeds of dogs have up to 220 million."

"Whoa," says a skinny boy with a mop of blond hair.

The boss nods. "So dogs can detect scents a lot better than we do."

While the boss explains how we search, Molly divides her time between watching him and staring at the door. I still have no idea what she's looking for, but after a bit I start to think that maybe another nap is in order. Then the boss calls Molly's name.

"Will you take Doodle outside for a minute while I hide these?" he says, retrieving the vials from the kids.

As soon as we're through the door and into the long hallway, Molly pulls her cell phone out of her pocket and punches it on. She keeps her eyes on it, her whole body tense, but finally sighs and snaps it shut.

Before long, the boss opens the door. "We're ready."

We go back into the room and Molly hands the leash to the boss.

"Okay." He smiles at the class. "Let's see what this sniffer dog can do. Doodle, find!" He stands back to let me search. I take a series of investigative sniffs. To quote that kid, *whoa.* Talk about scent overload. Between all of Molly's classmates, who by the smell of it had lunch not too long ago, and their parents who reek of coffee and car fumes and all sorts of things, a dog could sniff for a long time and not lose interest.

The boss gives a gentle tug on the leash. Oh yeah. Bed bugs. I get to work, concentrate on that one scent, and find them quickly. Molly, never without her camera, snaps photos while I work. The boss pays me with treats while the kids cheer and clap their hands. Hey, I could get used to this.

The teacher says a few more things and then a horrible buzzing makes me jump.

"That's the bell. Let's thank all our parents." The kids all clap. "Have a great weekend."

Chairs squeak and desks rattle as everyone stands up. Molly and I thread our way to the door, slowed by kids who come over to pet me and tell me how great I am. A few of the parents ask the boss for his business card. Beaming, he hands them out. He's happy, I'm happy, Molly's . . . Molly's not happy. I don't know why, but I can smell it on her plain as bacon. As soon as we get out into the hallway she turns her phone on and checks it again, her mouth tightening as she studies it for a minute.

The door to another classroom opens and kids swarm through the door. These kids are older, bigger and—hey! One of them is Kenny, Tanya's brother. Kenny plays ball with me when Molly and I are over at the Franklin's.

He comes over to give me a pat. "Justin, LaVon," he calls out to a couple of boys just coming out of the classroom down at the end of the hall. Both are as tall and thin as Kenny, one light-skinned while the other could be Kenny's brother. From looks, I mean, not smell.

"Meet my best bud, Doodle," Kenny says when they reach us. "I call him The Dude." Both friends reach down to pat me. I wag my tail. Have I mentioned this school of Molly's is a great place?

"What the—?" The pale guy stares at his cell phone. "We got cops doing a drug raid."

"Here?" Molly, Kenny, and the boss all say simultaneously.

But now that I think of it, I catch a scent. I raise my head and sniff again. My hair raises on my back. Drugs, specifically what my second boss—the bad one—called "weed." (He trained me to find his stash when he'd hidden it so well he couldn't find it himself.) I don't specialize in detecting drugs like some of my dog friends, but I gather that they're bad. Not to mention that where there's drugs, there's usually police. I look around. No police that I can see. But where is the scent coming from? I crinkle my nose, honing in—

"Doodle!" the boss says, with a slight jerk of the leash.

Oh. Guess I was pulling. Nothing the boss hates more than pulling. Well, except barking. And growling. Oh, and biting. Not that I've ever bitten anyone without good reason—even the boss admits that.

The pale boy steps back, suddenly anxious. "See ya in a few," he says to Kenny. "I gotta do something. Come on, LaVon." They hurry off just as a man emerges from Kenny's classroom down the hall and hurries straight toward us.

"Hey, Kenny," he says. The man's wearing a sports coat (which strangely men wear when they're not playing sports) and has a shiny gold watch that flashes when he moves his wrist. He smiles but his scent—mostly coffee, soap, pizza, and a trace of cologne—all overlaid with the acrid odor of nervous tension.

Kenny, a good head taller, smiles down at him. "Hey, Coach."

But the man's eyes are fixed on Kenny's friends now nearly to the end of the hall. The muscles in his jaw tighten as he watches them disappear around the corner. "Where they going?"

Kenny shrugs. "Practice, I think."

The man narrows his eyes, jaw still tight, and abruptly turns to Kenny. "Listen, I had something come up that I got to take care of right now. Go ahead and start drills. I'll be about a half an hour late to practice. Mr. Austin will take charge until I get there. Okay?"

"Sure, Coach," Kenny begins, but his coach is already half way to the exit.

"He's in a rush," the boss says.

Kenny laughs. "Coach Thatcher's always in a rush."

The boss says, "I guess I'd better go, too, or I might get caught in traffic." He grimaces and hands the leash to Molly. "Tell Mrs. Franklin I won't be able to make dinner after all. I have to drive out to Fairfax to do a quick estimate. I'll be back by 8 or 8:30 to pick you up."

We get to go to the Franklin's for dinner? This day just gets better and better!

"I could spend the night. So you wouldn't have to come and get me." Molly gives her dad a wheedling look.

He shakes his head. "We have practice at nine tomorrow. Remember? At Annie's house."

Molly sighs. Don't know why. She usually likes practice.

I watch him leave, then I lean against Kenny, hoping for another scratch behind the ears, but he suddenly straightens up.

Two cops, a man and a woman, stride briskly toward us.

"Bye, Dude." Kenny says. "See you tonight." He takes off at an angle from the cops.

Molly's phone beeps. She pulls it out, studies it a second, then says, "Tanya and her mom are already in the car. They must have gone out the side exit." She beeps some more keys, her eyes fixed on the display, then snaps it shut with unusual force. "She could have at least texted," she says. "Or left a message. How hard is that?"

I'm lost here since I thought she just heard from Tanya. But then I don't understand phones and never will. It's just not a dog thing.

Molly turns so abruptly I have to jump not to be yanked by the leash. But as I trot alongside her, I see the cops change direction so that they intercept Kenny.

"Kenny Franklin?" the woman cop says. "We need to talk to you for a minute."

I doubt Molly hears this—not just because we dogs have such better hearing than humans, but because her eyes are fixed on the exit.

But I hear it, and I see the surprise on his face change to fear as he asks, "What's going on?"

Now I wonder if he needs help. I move toward him, but Molly jerks the leash, something she rarely does, and says, "Doodle, come on."

Chapter 2

Cops!

I LOVE BEING AT THE FRANKLIN'S. THE FOOD'S GREAT and the Franklins aren't afraid to share it. I even have my own food dish and water bowl that Mrs. Franklin got for me after the shooting incident at the hotel, even though, according to the boss, the bullet just grazed me. She calls me her "substitute dog."

Today, Mr. Franklin grills hot dogs, a food I love despite the name. I mean, it's obvious by the smell and the shape that the food isn't really dog. I hang out in the backyard with him while he cooks. The Franklin's yard is even smaller than ours, and the grass grows in clumps surrounded by large patches of dirt. I find a spot in the farthest corner to relieve myself and leave my mark as a warning for the cats whose scents I detect. Then I help him keep an eye on the food in case any of those cats show up.

We go inside, Mr. Franklin carrying the fragrant platter of the meat, to find that Mrs. Franklin has put all sorts of other food on the table.

"Dinner," she shouts down the hall leading to the bedrooms.

Molly and Tanya come giggling down the hall, followed by Tanya's younger brother, Tyson, and then Derrin, the oldest of the Franklin boys. The chairs scrape on the wood floor—hurts my ears a little to be honest—as they find a place at the table.

But before she sits down to eat, Mrs. Franklin puts an entire hot dog and bun in my dish, along with a few globs of potato salad.

See what I mean? Never would happen if the boss were around. He says dogs should only eat dog food—that it's bad for them to eat human food. Can he really believe that? It's like saying cats shouldn't have claws. Or squirrels don't run if you chase them.

Molly grins up at her. "Dad would say you're spoiling him."

Mrs. Franklin laughs, her voice deep and low. "He don't have to know then."

"Kenny still at practice?" Mr. Franklin asks as he squirts ketchup onto several open buns. I like ketchup myself, mustard too, although mostly I like the meat they end up on. Mr. Franklin has short curly hair like mine except his is white. He's as lean as Mrs. Franklin is broad. He and all the Franklin boys smell like oil and gasoline because they fix cars.

"Don't know where he's at. They started early today so he ought to be home by now."

"Coach Thatcher said he was going to be late," Molly offers before biting into her hot dog.

I lick my bowl clean and stretch out for a nice nap when suddenly, through the dining room window, a light pulses on and off. Startled, I jump up and bark. Then remember what this particular light means. Cops. Now why would cops be here? I leap up sniffing for intruders. None that I can smell.

Mr. and Mrs. Franklin must be wondering the same thing because they rise from their chairs, their brows creased with alarm.

The doorbell rings. Mr. Franklin hurries to the front door. I rush ahead of him. Never know if I might be needed.

"Doodle! Back!"

I let Mr. Franklin push ahead of me. He opens the door to reveal Kenny and two other people on the porch.

"Lamar Franklin?" A woman wearing a cop's uniform holds up a badge. Beside her, a man, also in a police uniform, holds Kenny's arm. He's a good head shorter than Kenny; the woman shorter yet.

"I'm Detective Bennett," the woman says. She looks too small to be a cop. Of course, the only woman cop I've really met is Molly's mother, who has brown skin and black hair like mine, but straight, not curly. This cop has tufts of light colored hair sticking out from under her hat and gray eyes. The top of her head doesn't quite reach Kenny's shoulders.

There's something familiar about her. The man, too.

Both of them smell nervous, but that's not it. I take several deep sniffs and then remember—these are the cops who came up to Kenny at the school.

"I need to speak to you about Kenny," the woman says.

"Yes?" The fear and hostility in Mr. Franklin's voice makes me growl. And then I feel Molly's hand on my back. I hadn't heard her come up behind me.

"Hush," she whispers.

"We had an incident at Tri-State Science Academy. Drugs were found in Kenny's locker. May I come in and talk to you about it?"

"*Drugs?*" For a long moment, Mr. Franklin stares as if he can't understand what the cop just said. At last, his shoulders sag and he motions them in. "All right."

He turns to the faces of the entire family, who are watching wide-eyed. "Go finish your dinner," he says to the kids in a sharp voice while he holds the door open for the cops. Molly, Tanya, and Tyson slowly walk out, casting glances over their shoulders. Derrin hangs back, obviously wanting to stay. Me, I can't decide what to do. In the dining room there's always the chance for more food. But Mr. and Mrs. Franklin are so anxious that maybe they need guarding even though they could clearly beat these shorter cops in a fight. Except the cops have guns strapped to their belts. Guns can be a problem.

I take a position in the doorway, alert to sounds from either direction

"What's this about drugs?" Mr. Franklin asks. His voice rasps as if he's having trouble speaking.

Kenny gives his father an agonized glance. "Not mine, Dad. You know I don't do drugs. Any of it." Beads of sweat moisten his forehead.

The cop stands just inside the doorway. "Today we did a random drug search at Tri-State. We used dogs to sniff the lockers."

Dogs. I knew it. The nose never lies.

"One of our dogs found seven grams of marijuana in Kenny's locker."

Mr. Franklin nods, the rest of his body stiff. Mrs. Franklin stands like a statue beside her husband.

"Not mine, Dad. I swear it." Kenny sounds near tears. Too much emotion. I scratch my ear vigorously and then whine softly. And then I feel a hand on my back. Molly again. She stands on the other side of the door, out of sight from those in the living room, Tanya and Tyson next to her. She brings a finger to her lips.

"The reason that we're here," the cop continues, "is that we found enough that he could be selling it. The department is deciding whether or not to press charges."

Silence. Finally, Mr. Franklin speaks, his voice calm, his words deliberate. "So what do we need to do?"

"We have advised Kenny of his rights and it's up to you whether or not you'd like to get a lawyer. The school will be contacting you about this. But if I could ask a few questions, we might be able to clear this all up right now." She gives Mr. and Mrs. Franklin a sympathetic smile, as if to say she's on their side.

"Go ahead," Mrs. Franklin says, not returning the smile.

The cop shifts her weight and stares a second at the couch and chairs but no one invites her to sit down. She turns to Kenny. "You say these aren't your drugs?"

"No, man. I don't do that sh—" he glances at his mother—"that stuff. I play ball, you know? And make good grades."

Mrs. Franklin nods at that. "Straight A's. You can ask the school."

"Who else knows your locker combination?"

"No one," Kenny says. But then his forehead wrinkles as if he's suddenly remembering something. "No one," he repeats as if trying to convince himself.

The cop hears the change. "You sure?"

"No one." Kenny gives her a belligerent stare as if daring her to contradict him.

"Not a single one of your friends? Because if that pot really isn't yours, it's just plain stupid to take the rap for someone else. So I'm going to ask again, who else had the combination to your locker?"

Kenny shakes his head.

"This is a serious charge, one that could affect your life for a long time. If you're a straight-A student, then you're smart enough to understand this. Right? Who else, Kenny?"

"No one." Kenny's eyes take on the desperate look of a trapped animal. I hear a rumbling. Molly whispers, "Don't growl." Oh.

"Well, if you're the only one on the face of the earth who can get into the locker, the drugs have to be yours. It's as simple as that."

Kenny stares at his feet. Mrs. Franklin crosses over to him and puts an arm around his shoulder. "I think he's said all he's got to say."

The cop sighs. "Okay. I'm not going to keep him in custody right now, but that could change." Her partner holds the door open for her, but before she goes through, she turns back. "Don't be stupid, Kenny. Don't throw your life away for some pothead who's using you."

And then she's through the door and it slams behind her.

Chapter 3

The Mother. Again

After the cops leave, all the Franklins and even Molly are so upset that no one finishes their food. Which works out well for me because I get a lot of leftovers in my dish. Still, I'm glad when the boss pulls up in the van. Too much emotion in that house.

But the boss watches with a face as gloomy as any of the Franklins while Molly puts me in my crate. So the van offers no escape from all this sadness after all.

As soon as we're on the road, the boss starts to tap the steering wheel, something he does when he's anxious or excited. "Molly—"

But she interrupts him. "Did you hear about Kenny?" He shakes his head and she tells him all about the cop and the pot—a funny name I've always thought since marijuana doesn't look or, more to the point, *smell* anything like a pot. Or a pan, for that matter.

By the time she finishes, we're pulling into the driveway. "I know he didn't do it,"

The boss's fingers rap on the wheel. "Either way, it's a mess." He turns off the engine but makes no move to get out.

"Molly—" He clears his throat.

"Yeah?" Molly unclicks her seatbelt and opens the door.

"I got a phone message today. From your mother."

Molly's arm drops to her side, the door still open. "She's canceling?" Her voice is laced with fear.

The boss seems taken aback. "Canceling?"

"My visit on the 18th. I *knew* she wouldn't go through with it. Especially after today." Whoa. Her voice is so bitter that I feel a sudden urge to scratch. Not to mention I have other urges that I need to take care of. It's been a long time since anyone thought to put me outside. But Molly doesn't budge.

"She didn't call about that." He takes a deep breath. "She asked me to tell you that she got caught in a case and couldn't make it to career day." The boss pauses as if to let his words sink in. "I didn't know she was invited."

After a bit, Molly says in a small voice, "I called her."

"Moll." The boss scrunches up his face, and then sighs. "You asked her without telling me? If it were a parent-teacher conference or some kind of achievement award—something to do with you—"

"She has a career, too."

"And you don't think I wouldn't have found it awkward to be in the middle of a demonstration with Doodle and have my ex-wife whom I haven't seen in almost seven years walk in?"

Uh-oh. He's angry now. Molly bites her lip. Cold air rushes in through the van's open door but neither seems to notice it.

"Doesn't matter. She didn't make it anyway." She turns her face to the window. "Anyway, you saw her a few weeks ago at the hotel. When Doodle got shot."

I scratch my side, testing the skin where the bullet grazed me. Still doing well.

"Molly, you know what I mean. Before that. Seven *years* she couldn't be bothered to contact us." He shuts his eyes, as if remembering. "Moll." He shakes his head. "I … I don't want you to be hurt and this thing with your mother … it's … she's … going to hurt you. I know it."

"I'm sorry," Molly says, and I hear the quaver in her words. But she swallows and says in a firm voice, "I should have told you. I did it—called her—on the spur of the moment. She's a cop. The kids would like that. And I thought …" Her voice trembles and her fists tighten. "I thought if she could see you with Doodle she might remember … she might miss … being with you."

The boss's eyes widen in dismay. "Oh, Moll," he says, his voice falling as if he's heard really sad news. "Oh, Moll …" He's silent for a long time. "Her and me—you have to know that will never happen. It's just not possible. Too much has gone on." He rubs his beard. "Too much. Do you understand? That will *never* happen. Maybe you can have some kind of relationship with her—I have to be honest and say I doubt it, but maybe. But us together again will never happen. Never."

Molly nods.

For a moment, neither speak. Then the boss says, "We'd better get inside or we'll catch pneumonia."

I've never figured out what this pneumonia thing is that people always worry about catching. Best I can tell, it's not something good like a ball or a Frisbee.

Molly nods again, gets out, pulls open the sliding door and unlatches my crate. I jump out, give a quick shake, and touch my nose to her hand.

The mother again. I've only met her once, and that turned out to be complicated what with guns going off and everything.

Molly's mother is an undercover cop, a job I learned has nothing to do with blankets. She seemed nice enough to me, but for some reason she always makes Molly sad.

I move out of the way as the boss goes over to Molly and pulls her into an awkward hug. "Just be careful, okay? About hoping too much? You can't control what other people feel. Or do." He sighs. "Seven years, remember. Don't expect too much from the visit."

"I know," she says. She leads me through the side gate. At last!

But when she bends to unclip the leash, I see her cheeks are wet with tears. So I pause to lick her hand before I rush off to do what the boss likes to call my "business."

When we go back inside, the boss is at his desk. He mumbles something about doing paperwork. No clue why he calls it that since all he does is sit in front of his computer and uses hardly any paper at all. But Molly must have paperwork, too, because when we go to her room, she sits down at her computer and doesn't budge. Nothing for me to do but take a nap. Which I do until the boss raps on the door.

"Yeah." Molly's still in front of her computer.

The boss leans in through the opening. "Don't stay up too late. We have to leave by 8:30 to be at Annie's by 9."

Molly's yawn turns into a frown. "Why so early?"

"Sid Berkshire's coming with the crew that does the set up for the NABBS certification. They're going to hide the vials and rate each dog, just like it'll be in the actual trial. So it'll be great practice."

Molly yawns again. "Do we have to go?"

"With the trial less than a month away? I don't see how we can miss."

According to the boss, the NABBS test is a big deal because the dogs that pass it get a certification to prove that their "finds" are accurate. Typical of humans not to trust our noses, but don't get me going on that.

He likes to say the certification will mean Josh Hunter Detection is more than just a guy with a dog and a business license and we'll get more "big time" jobs, in the ritzy hotels around Arlington and DC.

"Okay," Molly says, turning back to her computer.

"So, you'll get to bed soon?"

"Yeah." Molly sounds annoyed.

"Good night, then. Don't forget to brush your teeth." The boss closes the door.

True to her word, Molly shuts down the computer, goes off to the bathroom to do her teeth, and then crawls under the covers. I curl down on the rug beside her bed. I used to have to sleep in my crate, but since we had a break-in the boss lets me sleep in Molly's room. Have to say I prefer it even though I don't sleep quite as well since I need to be on the alert for any noise or scent from intruders.

Tonight, though, it's not intruders that wake me up. It's the sound of Molly crying into her pillow.

Chapter 4

Dead Bugs

I LOVE GOING TO ANNIE'S HOUSE. SHE HAS A HUGE yard, much bigger than the tiny one at our place. A dog could find lots of great places to relieve himself in this yard and as soon as I'm out of the van I can tell that many have, including some I don't know.

"Doodle, don't *pull.*"

Oh.

We don't go up to the front door, but head around to the side gate as usual. As soon as the boss has latched the gate behind us, Annie shouts, "Doodle!" and squats down, arms wide open.

Molly unclips the leash and I race across the expanse of grass, now half-covered in leaves, and skid to a stop in front of Annie. I sit up, my paws in the air.

This always makes her laugh. Annie smells like treats, cheese, coffee, and some kind of soap. And dogs, of course, because of her job with Miguel, the man who trained me to find bed bugs. Today, she has her hair pulled back under a hat, and is wearing jeans and a flannel shirt. She gives me a broad smile. "Doodle, you're such a character."

Don't know what she means by that, but I don't care. Annie gives me several *very* tasty treats from a pouch she wears around her waist. I wish the boss would get that kind. I decide to go greet the other dogs, but Annie grabs hold of my collar until Molly comes and reattaches the leash.

While everyone is talking, I stick up my nose and do a little air sampling. Lots of interesting scents here from the group. Besides Annie and her beagle, Chloe, there's a male beagle who is here with a stocky, dark-haired man who smells faintly of garlic, a female Labrador with a thin, intense man who reeks of cigarette smoke, and another beagle, male, with a tall woman whose toothy smile reminds me somehow of horses, but who carries the scent of several dogs and, unfortunately, cats.

A long, covered porch runs the length of the house. We join the group at the closer end, where plastic chairs on the cement floor surround a long wooden picnic table. At the far end of the porch are some couches, stuffed chairs and tables all on a large square of carpet. This is the area where the vials will be hidden, at least if they run the practice the same way as last time. Molly pulls out her camera and snaps a few photos.

Annie startles me by waving an arm and calling out, "Hey, Jerry. Over here." A heavyset man and a German shepherd plod their way across the lawn.

"Everyone, this is Jerry Arlen and his dog, Gunther. Jerry, this is—" she rattles off the names of everyone, but I'm more interested in Gunther.

It's no secret that dogs can read body language. We pretty much know how anyone near us feels simply by the way they stand and move. Which is how I know Gunther doesn't like his boss. The way he carries his tail in a low, almost timid way.

The way he keeps his head down. All this tells me that Gunther is one unhappy German shepherd.

His boss, Jerry, nods at everyone as he sinks down onto the bench, wheezing slightly.

Annie raps a spoon against a tin cup. "Attention, everyone. We need to get started." The conversation quiets to a low murmur. "I'd like to introduce Sid Berkshire, who has graciously offered to come and set up today's practice. Sid's the new manager for Smithfield's Sniffer Dogs over in Fairfax, where the next NABBS trial will be held."

A muscular man dressed in a tight shirt tucked into tight jeans, shiny boots, and a bright yellow jacket, nods and smiles at the group. Sunlight glints off a single earring, along with the gold chain around his neck. I've seen these kinds of chains before. At first I wondered if humans had to have collars like we do, but it turns out they just wear them to dress up, kind of like when I get my coat brushed and wear my vest for work.

"Thanks, Annie. Good to see you all here. Not all business owners realize how important certification can be to the future of their company. The money spent in proper training and in gaining certification establishes you as a serious professional who has met industry standards and whose results can be trusted."

While he's speaking, a few more people and dogs come in through the side gate and join the group.

"But you already know that or you wouldn't be here. Today's practice should give you a good indication of how your dog will do at the trials. If your dog does great, just keep doing the same thing in your practices. And if your dog does less than great—" he raises his eyebrows as he gives a rueful chuckle

"—don't panic. There's still time to remedy the situation. Over at Smithfield's, we specialize in turning around dogs who aren't performing quite up to standard."

Sid waves at two men wearing baseball caps, standing off to the side. "Ramón and Steven here will set up the course. For the actual event, to ensure the integrity of the test, the courses will be set up by two law enforcement officers who have logged over 1,000 hours experience with scent detection dogs."

With that, he gestures to Annie, who holds up a plastic bowl. "I've put a slip with the names of every team here," she says. "We'll draw to see what the order will be." She shakes the bowl and Sid reaches in and pulls out a piece of paper.

"Josh Hunter and Doodle," he announces. He continues to read off a list of names while the two men set up a series of folding screens in front of furniture where the vials will be hidden. They disappear behind the screens.

"Ready, Doodle?" Molly pats my head and hands my leash over to the boss, who takes it in one hand, rubbing his beard with the other.

I have no idea why he's nervous. Maybe it's because of all the beagles. The boss is always saying that beagles make some of the best sniffer dogs. But I've proven my nose is as good as any other's over and over again, which Molly remembers even if the boss doesn't. Which is why she's smiling and much more relaxed than the boss. She knows I always get my bug, so to speak. The boss could learn from her.

Ramón and Steven fold back the screens. "Ready," one of them says. The boss leads me over to the furniture, strokes his beard and gives the command. "Find."

I start sniffing the area around the chairs. Hmm. I crinkle my nose. Along with the cigarette smell—someone sat here and smoked—wafts the distinct odor of pizza. Love pizza myself, though the boss doesn't often give it to me.

The boss sighs in the way that means he's getting impatient, and even Molly gives me a nod as if to say, "Hurry up."

So I ignore the pizza and nervous sweat and the more enjoyable odors from the dogs and move to the padded chairs and sofa that all sit on a big square of carpet, searching for that one distinct scent.

The first chair I pass is clean, other than a plastic-like smell to the cover which all the furniture seems to have. Ditto for the second. I cast about some more. The couch now—hey, chips! I'm a big fan of chips, another food the boss is stingy with. If I nudge the cushion just a bit . . . But wait. I smell bed bug also—very faint. If I'm right, the little glass vial is just under this end of the cushion. I nose in closer.

No, wait. Hah. Almost caught me. Those are dead bugs. What the boss calls distractors, put there to try to fool us dogs. Most people wouldn't think there's a difference in smell between live and dead bugs—but then humans are practically blind to scents.

I cast about until I catch a whiff of bed bugs, live ones this time. I glance at the boss. He stands straight and stares at the wall with what he calls his poker face, an expression I don't understand at all. He does this when I'm searching so he doesn't inadvertently train me to find the bugs by watching him instead of using my nose. His words, not mine, but the point is he tries not to give me any help. Doesn't always succeed, especially when he's hidden the bugs himself. Poker face or not, humans don't realize how much they tell us without meaning to.

I snort a little to clear out my nose and circle closer and closer to the scent—which turns out to be in a thinly cushioned chair. Nothing on the legs or the back, but under here—I lift the cushion with my nose and take a deep sniff. Bingo, as the boss sometimes says. I sit and point with my nose. I hear the click of Molly's camera as she snaps a picture.

"*Good* boy, Doodle. Good job." The boss gives me a big smile as he pays me with a tasty liver treat that's almost as good as the ones Annie has.

I continue to search and find a vial taped to the underside of a table, and then the last one under a corner of carpet.

But, as the boss is paying me for the last find, Sid holds up the vial his assistant just handed him. "Sorry. These are dead ones." He gives the boss a sympathetic smile.

I don't think so. The bugs I found were alive. I'd bet my nose on it. Although—I raise my nose and sniff at the vial that Sid is holding out. Dead ones there, yes but that's not the vial I found. At least I don't think it is.

"What?" the blood has drained from the boss's face. "He's never done a false alert before. Ever."

Sid shrugs. "It happens. Could be the stress of the event. Or it could be you've been giving him clues all along. Not consciously, of course."

"But we've done plenty of trials where I don't know where the vials are." He shakes his head.

"Well—" Sid gestures to the others—"and this goes for all of you—this is what this run through is for—to see real results.

You can deny them or you can do something about them. Up to you."

Now the boss's color deepens. Anger flows off him as plain as smoke from a fire. He leads me back without a word, and drops into a chair beside Molly.

But she throws her arms around my neck. "I believe you," she whispers, slipping a hand with a treat up to my mouth when the boss isn't looking. I swallow it quickly before he sees. "Something's wrong, isn't it, Doodle?"

Certainly is. I found live bed bugs, then they were dead, and now the boss glowers first at Sid and then at me as if we're both his worst enemies.

Something is very wrong indeed.

Chapter 5

Gunther Gets a Treat

NOT SURE WHAT'S GOING ON WITH MOLLY. SHE moves over to one of the plastic lawn chairs and stands behind it. I jump up to follow her, but she shakes her head and flashes a hand signal that means "Sit—Stay."

Okay. I sit. She bends over and fumbles. At first, I think she's getting me a treat for sitting, but instead she eases her camera from the case, holding it low, pointing it at Annie's beagle, Chloe, who is up next. Chloe finds all her bugs quickly and makes no mistakes.

"What a *good* girl," Annie says, feeding her several treats that I can smell from the length of the porch, while the boss, head down, stares dejectedly at his lap.

And speaking of treats—I edge forward and give Molly a look to remind her that I'm still sitting and staying *very* nicely. But her eyes—and her camera—are fixed on the Labrador retriever who's now searching. But here's the thing. Whenever either Sid or the handler looks in her direction, Molly whisks the camera behind the chair. What's with that? And she's forgotten about my Sit-Stay. I give up and lie down.

The Labrador finds all her vials with no false alerts. But when the horse-faced woman's beagle has his turn, he alerts twice on vials that turn out to have dead bugs. "He's never done that before," she says, as shocked and dismayed as the boss was earlier.

"Jerry Arlen and Gunther," Sid calls out. Jerry lumbers up and with an entirely unnecessary jerk on the leash, leads Gunther over to the furniture.

As before, Molly raises the camera and rests it on the edge of the chair.

"Find," Jerry commands in a tight, nervous voice. Sweat rolls down his puffy cheeks. He wears a crumpled shirt tucked into a pair of wrinkled pants so tight around his vast stomach that the button seems dangerously close to spiraling off. Which could be interesting. I haven't eaten a button since my puppy days, but I'm always open to the idea.

But more interesting is the way Gunther keeps casting wary glances back at his boss even as he sniffs the air for clues. As if he's looking to his boss for help, something a boss should never do. I mean the whole point of having a bed bug dog is that the dogs, with their infinitely superior noses, are the ones who do the finding.

But Gunther doesn't seem to trust his nose. Maybe that's why the sweat keeps rolling down Jerry's cheeks even though all the humans are wearing wind breakers and the air vibrates with the smell of newly fallen leaves. Gunther sniffs and sniffs and eyes his boss with increasing alarm, but he never gives the alert that signals a find.

The flush on his boss's face deepens and now I can smell his anger.

"Find," he repeats, sounding as if he has a bone in his throat.

Poor Gunther sniffs and circles some more and finally gives an alert by sitting and pointing with his nose. I feel a few of the humans sigh with relief. His boss turns toward us, relief spreading on his face. But it's short-lived.

"Sorry." Sid holds up a vial. Dead ones."

Jerry's chest swells and the button strains even more. I watch with interest. "I can't afford that. Already spent a fortune training this—" here, he uses a word the boss calls *language* "—dog." He glowers down at Gunther who shrinks back and doesn't meet his gaze. No treat for him.

"Find!" Jerry practically shouts. Gunther slinks away from him and begins to sniff, but clearly he's more worried about his boss than about what's in front of his nose.

Annie clears her throat. "I'm not sure this is doing Gunther any go—"

Jerry gives no sign that he hears this. "Find!" he repeats, his voice so harsh that I have to scratch my ear. And then, for some reason, he throws a quick glance back in our direction. And stops. He whirls around and jabs a finger at Molly. "Hey, what're you doing?"

Molly shoves the camera in her jacket pocket, but she's too late. "You're taking *photos*? Gonna make fun of me on Facebook?" He strides toward her, his face contorted in anger.

I don't think so. In a flash, I'm between him and Molly. I'd like to growl and bare my teeth, but the boss gets *really* upset when I do. So I just block his way and when he tries to move around me, I block him again.

"Damn dog." His booted foot hurtles toward me, but I'm too quick for him. I sidle out of the way and then back in front of Molly.

Now everyone's shouting and all the beagles begin barking wildly. My boss pushes between me and Jerry. "Hey, slow down. What's going on?"

"She has no *right* to photograph me."

The boss doesn't seem to hear. "You tried to kick my dog."

"He was going to bite me."

"I didn't—" the boss begins.

But Annie interrupts him. She draws herself up and with the energy of a Rottweiler staring down an intruder, she says in a cold, commanding voice, "It doesn't matter what he was doing. No one can treat dogs that way at my home. *Ever*. No matter what the provocation."

Whoa. Tough as well as nice. Didn't know she had it in her.

Although she kind of ruins the effect when she bends down and whispers, "Chloe, *hush*!" Chloe stops barking and the other owners quiet their dogs too.

Jerry, still blustering says, "I wasn't going to *touch* him. Just to get him to move."

Yeah, right.

Now Sid pushes forward. "Hey, hey, let's all calm down." He gives a little laugh that sounds anything but calm, and the color has drained from his face. "It's natural for emotions to run high at these things. A lot at stake, for all of us."

He smiles down at Molly, who shrinks back a bit.

"Young lady, I bet you're quite the photographer."

Jerry starts, "But she had no right—"

Sid raises a hand. "Just let me finish." He turns back to Molly. "I want to apologize to you. I should have made it clear to Annie and, um, Josh, is it? And to everyone—" he waves at the group, "that in these events that we set up, we never allow any kind of photographs. Gets us in all sorts of problems with the suits, know what I mean?"

No clue here, and Jerry must see the blank looks on some of the humans because he adds, "Lawyers and insurance people. Always making life complicated, right?" Another tense laugh.

He smiles down at Molly."I know you're too young to understand any of that." He holds his hands up as if it's beyond him, too. "But trust me. I'd be in big trouble if any of these photographs got out. So I need you to delete them."

He tugs a wallet from the pocket of his jeans and makes a big show of lifting out a bill.

"How 'bout I trade you this ten for erasing those photos?"

Molly, white-faced, stares at him as if she doesn't understand.

"A little reward for the time spent taking them," Sid adds.

Molly doesn't move.

The boss turns to her. "Molly?"

Without a word, she pulls the camera from her pocket, turns away from Sid, hunching over it for a minute or so as she presses some buttons. Then she flips it around and holds it out toward Sid.

"It's erasing."

He squints at the screen for a second, then smiles, relief pouring off him.

"Great. Wonderful. I knew you'd understand." He flaps the bill at her hand. "Here."

"No thanks." Molly's face floods with color. She shoves the camera back in her pocket.

"Sure?" When Molly shakes her head, Sid pockets the money. "Your choice. So, we're all good now? Annie? Jerry?"

Jerry gives a tight-lipped nod to Annie, who says, "Okay," in a voice that sounds anything but.

"Good. Whew!" Sid gives an exaggerated sigh of relief. "Who's up next?" He pulls a slip of paper from the bowl and calls out a name.

But my eye is on Annie, who's doling out treats to Chloe. I move toward her as far as the leash will allow and sit very nicely.

She laughs. "Doodle, you're a card." She gives me two of those marvelous treats. I wag my tail in appreciation. I have to say that Annie has quite a pleasant scent to her. Not as great as Molly's, but then no one has a scent as great as Molly's.

And then, she turns to Gunther, who's watching with interest. "I guess we shouldn't leave you out."

"Hey, don't do that." Jerry's harsh voice stops Annie just as she's about to give a treat to Gunther. "You'll spoil him and he won't work."

Gunther, his nose up in anticipation, begins to drool at the treat now held halfway between him and Annie.

"I don't think one dog biscuit—" Annie begins, but Jerry interrupts her.

"My trainer was very clear. He only gets fed when he works. I didn't pay a fortune for this dog to have his training ruined." He scowls at Annie who slowly pulls her hand back and slips the biscuit into the treat pouch. Poor Gunther's drool now reaches almost to the floor.

"Gunther, down!"

No dog would want to obey that boss. Not the way his voice and his body practically shout his anger. But Gunther pauses for only a fraction of a second before he drops to the floor and lays his head on his paws.

I hear Molly's breath catch.

Jerry wipes his forehead with a handkerchief. "I don't want to be harsh, but I'm new to all this. I have to follow my trainer's instructions. Otherwise this investment will all be—" he points his thumb at the ground.

"Who is your trainer?" Annie asks.

"Originally J. R. Hosteler. In Maryland. Do you know him?"

"I'm afraid not," she says. A curious phrase that people use when they're not actually afraid.

"He's supposed to be good. But now … Sid says I can work with him but he's very expensive. All this dog stuff—if I'd known how hard it is … my health is not what it was…" he dabs his forehead again. "But never mind." He flushes as if embarrassed by what he's revealed. "Do you have a bathroom I could use?"

"Sure. Through that door, in the right hand corner of the kitchen."

He hefts himself up from the bench then starts to tie the leash around the leg of the table.

"I'll hold him if you like," Annie says.

"Oh, yes, thank you." He passes the leash to her and lumbers to the door.

As soon as it closes behind him, Molly says, "Poor Gunther."

"Yeah," Annie agrees. "I read a study that says dogs notice if other dogs get treats and they get left out. They get jealous."

Well, duh.

Sid calls out another name, and a dog and handler I don't recognize move over to the arena.

With a furtive glance toward the door, Molly goes over to Gunther and strokes his head.

“You’re a good boy, aren’t you?” She massages the top of his neck. Then stops a second and frowns. “Is that a—” She feels around his collar. “Oh.” Her face darkens. “I thought it might be a tick on his neck. But it’s a scab.”

Annie bends over and checks his neck. “Some people should never be allowed to use a prong collar,” she says darkly. She reaches into her pocket, giving Molly a questioning look.

Molly puts a finger to her mouth. “Mum’s the word.”

“Here you go.” She offers him a treat. Gunther swallows it in a single gulp. I prefer to chew my food, but to each his own. She gives him another. Hey! Am I going to get more too?

I guess not. Annie’s hands stay away from the pouch. When Jerry comes back outside, they’re folded serenely on her lap.

He takes the leash. “Thank you.” Then, turning to Molly, he says “Sorry, didn’t mean to yell at you. This test means a lot to me—I get . . . nervous. A big investment, this dog. My business depends on him. Forgive me?”

Molly mumbles something unintelligible but Jerry seems to take it as agreement.

“Come on, Gunther,” he says. And with Gunther, head and tail low, at his heels, he makes his way slowly toward the gate.

Chapter 6

Hatching a Plan

IN THE VAN, AS THE BOSS SNAPS ON HIS SEATBELT, HE says, "That Annie, she's something. She just stood down Jerry like she was twice his size. No wonder she gets such good results from Chloe. She's got 'It' in spades."

He starts tapping the steering wheel. "Not to mention she's got looks and personality. I should farm Doodle out to her. I bet she could whip him into shape."

"It,"according to the boss is a mysterious force some dog trainers have that make dogs automatically inclined to obey them. Sometimes he uses the word "energy" to mean the same thing. The boss often claims if only he had "it" I'd be a better dog. I doubt it. Work for a wage, that's my motto, as I've mentioned before. That said, there's no denying, some trainers have more of a gift for communication than others. I mean, with some people, even if you *want* to obey, you can't figure out what they're asking.

He taps some more. "You know, that's not a bad idea. Maybe she can fix Doodle's false alert problem."

Molly says, "I don't believe Doodle gave a false alert. Something was wrong."

I'll say. Quite can't figure out what though.

The boss sighs. "I hope so. Maybe there was some other scent there that confused him. Annie said not to worry about it, that even the best dogs will occasionally have a false alert. Let's hope she's right."

Molly takes a drink from the water bottle she always has in van. "I don't like Sid. Kind of creepy."

"Definitely a salesman in the most negative sense of the word," the boss agrees.

"Annie says Miguel doesn't think much of his training school." He begins to tap again, the beat faster and louder. Then his fingers are still. He darts a glance at Molly. "Speaking of Annie…" His voice now has that fake enthusiasm that tells me he's nervous. "I hope you don't mind, but I invited her to come to dinner on Friday."

As soon as Molly answers, which isn't right away, I know she's not happy with the suggestion. "At *our* house?"

For once, even the boss notices it. Another darting glace. The tapping dies away. "Yeah. You don't like the idea?"

Molly shrugs. "I guess it's okay."

"I thought you liked Annie." This comes out sounding annoyed and Molly slumps down a little in her seat.

"I do. It's just that…" her voice trails away. "At our house…"

"Just that what?"

"Nothing," she repeats.

It takes a long time before the boss responds. Finally, he says, "Moll, your mother and me—like I said before—it's never going to happen."

Molly nods and doesn't speak again for the rest of the way home.

When we get out of the van, she takes me straight to her room. I nap—it's been a busy day—while she studies photos on her computer. At one point, I hear Sid's voice and jump up, but it's coming from her screen. Why it's a little movie of our practice. I watch Gunther alert on the vial, and see Sid hold it up. "Sorry, these are dead ones."

Molly clicks some keys and the scene goes backwards and then moves forward again. "Do you see how he's waving around that vial? How do we know the bugs are even dead? Just because he told us? I wonder if anyone actually checked?"

"Checked what?" The door swings open and the boss looms in the frame. Both Molly and I jump. Don't know why I didn't hear him.

"What's this?" He comes into the room and squints at the screen. "I thought you erased the card."

Molly flushes, bites her lower lip, and then says, "I archived all the videos first so they didn't erase."

From the expression on her face, she expects the boss to be angry, but instead his mouth slowly spreads into a smile. "No wonder you didn't take the money. You out-conned the con."

He laughs and then so does she, and I can't help but wag my tail. Nice to have everyone happy.

"It didn't seem right," she agrees, clearly relieved at his response. "I wanted to see if Sid, um Mr. Berkshire—was doing something to make the dogs fail. Because I don't believe Doodle made a mistake. But if he's doing something, I can't see it. Gunther's owner is mean, so maybe that's just his problem.

"Mean?" The boss raises his eyebrows and Molly tells him about finding the scabs on Gunther's neck.

"I believe it," the boss says when she finishes. "Anyone who'd kick a dog..." he looks over at me. "Not that I haven't been tempted, mind you, after *the barkster* here wakes up the whole neighborhood."

No clue what he's talking about except that it must involve me, because Molly throws her arms around my neck. "He's doing better now," she says.

"Because we keep him indoors. But the point is, anyone who'd kick a dog, tempted or not, shouldn't be a handler."

I couldn't agree more.

Molly gets up and goes back to her computer. "Can Tanya come over tomorrow?" Molly asks. "After church?" Her voice takes on that pleading tone she uses when she's trying to persuade the boss to do something he's reluctant to do. "We can go over our homework together."

But the boss doesn't need persuading. "Sure. She can stay for dinner. I imagine Lamar and Barbara have enough on their minds with Kenny that they won't miss her. How does Zeke's sound?"

"Great!" Molly says, echoing my own feelings. Zeke's is one of our favorite places. The boss says their burgers are the best anywhere in the DC area. I don't know about that—all burgers taste equally delicious to me, but I love Zeke's because it has seating outside and I can go along if it's not raining or too cold. And Molly always slips me bites of her burger. When she and the boss go to other places, where dogs aren't allowed, the most I get out of it is the scent of burgers and fries on their clothing.

So the next day, which I'm happy to see isn't rainy or cold, the Franklins pull up in their car, a van sort of like ours but shorter and darker. Tanya jumps out while the boss, careful to keep me behind the screen door, walks out to talk to Mr. Franklin.

"I was sorry to hear about Kenny," I hear him say, as I follow Tanya to Molly's room.

As soon as we're both inside, Molly shuts the door and I hear the click as she locks it. She taps some buttons on her computer and suddenly music is playing. Always startles me when she does that.

"So my dad doesn't hear," Molly says. "So, what's going on with Kenny?"

Tanya, usually bright and happy, now seems wrapped in sadness. I can smell the worry pouring from her. "Nothing new, really. Dad thinks Kenny's protecting a friend—probably Justin. He says that kid always looked like a pothead to him."

I picture a kid with a pot on his head, even though I suspect they mean something else.

"We know he gave his combination to someone. But he won't say who. My dad says that's practically as stupid as doing drugs."

Molly sighs. "We got to find out who put it in his locker."

"How we gonna do that? No one in seventh grade is going to talk to us."

Molly nods agreement and while they discuss it, I curl up on the nice fluffy rug that Molly has at the foot of her bed and take a nap. I wake up when Molly says in an excited voice, "Doodle!"

Still half-dreaming, I raise my head and peer at her sleepily. She and Tanya are munching on M&Ms—how'd I sleep through that? I sit up, interested, but the truth is that Molly never gives me chocolate. That doesn't stop me from drooling, though.

"Doodle could find it just like he finds bed bugs!"

Find what? M& Ms?

"Can he do that?" Tanya asks. "Does he know how to find pot?"

Oh, pot again. I lie back down.

"He hasn't been trained for it, but I bet it wouldn't be hard to teach him. He's really smart."

I have to agree there. My former service dog boss used to say I had the poodle smarts but it was too bad I got the poodle attitude along with it. But, I've said before, smart and obedient don't always go hand in hand.

Molly pops a few more candies in her mouth. "*Eeuuuw*, Doodle." She grabs a tissue and wipes a line of drool from my chin. "Thing is, I think I could train him. But I'd need some pot to do it. He has to know what scent he's going after."

Silence. Their eyes widen as if they're thinking about something scary.

"How could we get some?" Tanya asks in a hushed voice. "If we start asking around—I think if my dad heard I was askin' 'bout drugs after everything with Kenny . . . I don't know what he'd do, but it'd be *bad*."

"I don't know." Molly shakes her head. "What about Travis—what's his last name? In sixth grade?"

"Travis Duncan?"

"Yeah. I heard that he almost got kicked out of school last spring. He might know."

But now Tanya is shaking her head. "Kicked out of school is what we'll be if we start this. Why don't you ask your mom? She's a cop. I bet they have a whole storeroom full of it at the police station.

"I don't know." Molly frowns as she thinks about it. "She didn't even—"

But then there are footsteps outside and the boss raps on the door. "Anyone for burgers?" he asks.

"Yeah," Molly and Tanya say together. Molly hits a button on the computer and then opens the door. I push forward to remind them that I like burgers, too.

We have a great dinner at Zeke's. Molly gives me some fries and a piece of her hot dog and Tanya gives me a large chunk of her burger. And lots of people come over to pet me which is okay because I'm not wearing my work vest. I enjoy it, and the boss likes it because he can tell people how I find bed bugs and sometimes even hand out his cards.

Then we drop Tanya off. At home, after I get my time in the backyard, Molly brings me in. I'm just about to curl up on the rug when Molly sits on the floor beside me. She drapes an arm over my neck. "What do you think, Doodle? Should I ask her?"

Ask who what? I tilt my head trying to understand her better.

"On the plus side," she continues, "my mom could probably get the pot, no problem. And we wouldn't have to ask someone like Travis.

"On the minus side, she'd probably tell my dad and then we'd really be in trouble."

I yawn. I'd like to lie down, but Molly's arm still grips my neck.

"I mean, she didn't even call me when she couldn't come. She called him."

Her body stiffens. What's this? Tears well up in her eyes. "She didn't even call *me*, Doodle. And I bet she cancels my visit. I bet she does."

I am not normally one to lick humans. In my world, licking often means submission (or there's something tasty to be had) and, as I think I've said before, I like to keep things on a "do the job, get paid" basis and skip all this master/slave stuff. But there's something about Molly looking so sad that makes me lick the tears from her face.

"Oh, Doodle," she says, swiping a hand across her eyes, and giving the barest trace of a smile. "*You* understand."

Not sure I do, but when she gives me a final squeeze and then crawls into bed, I feel much the same way as when I find bed bugs. As if I had a job to do and did it well.

Chapter 7

An Unexpected Threat

One of the bad things about Molly being in school is that she doesn't go to work with us during the day. Frankly, the jobs are always more fun when she's along. Which is why I'm glad we're picking her up this afternoon to go to a job even though the boss and I did an apartment complex in the morning.

"Sorry," the boss says when Molly climbs into the van, a quizzical look on her face. He hands her a peanut butter sandwich and an apple. "We have to run out to do an estimate. The owner wanted to be there herself, and couldn't make it before four."

Peanut butter fumes waft through the van, and I start to drool even though there's no way I'll get any of the sandwich. Not with me in the crate and the boss right there.

But Molly surprises me. When we've stopped and she's getting me out, she bends over me and slides a hand with a crust of sandwich up to my mouth. Mostly bread but enough peanut butter to make it good. I swallow it whole so as not to give her away.

A light rain mists the sidewalks. Because of the chilly weather, the boss and Molly wear what they call wind-breakers—odd term—that have pictures on the back of a bed bug in a circle with a line drawn through it. I have the same picture on my vest.

The trees have shed half their leaves, which lie in fragrant piles along the curb, the rest waving damply from the branches. The air has that pleasant, smoky, wood-fire smell that always happens this time of year.

"Waddell Retirement Homes," Molly reads on a big sign that faces the street.

The boss says, "They have 130 units here, and something like 600 if you count their other locations. So it'd be a big job if we can get it."

Molly snaps a photo of the sign and the front of the building.

"No photos inside," the boss warns. "Remember what happened last time."

Which time? Molly's camera has gotten her in trouble more than once.

Molly's lips tighten for a second. "Okay." She drops the camera back into the pocket of her windbreaker. "Can I take Doodle?"

The boss hands her the leash. We walk over a broad sidewalk that's a little slick with rain and moss through the doors to the office. A paunchy, gray-haired man with glasses bends over the reception desk talking to—hey, it's Sid. Once again he's wearing tight jeans and tight shirt, which is open at the chest exposing tufts of light brown hair.

"Sid." The boss sounds more surprised than friendly.

"Hey, Josh. How's it going?" Sid smoothes the sides of his hair. A sharp cologne wafts from him, overwhelming all the other scents in the room. Molly wrinkles her nose. You know a scent is strong when humans can detect it. I hope I don't have to search for bugs right here.

"And how's my pretty little photographer doing today?" He reaches to pat Molly on the head. She backs away. She hates having her head patted, a sentiment I share. I move in front of her protectively.

"No more unauthorized photo sessions, I hope." His laugh has a threatening quality that makes my hair rise.

Molly mumbles something while the boss hands a paper to the clerk behind the desk.

"—an appointment to do an estimate," the boss is saying.

The clerk nods. "Mrs. Carter called and said she'd be a few minutes late."

"You too?" Sid laughs and lightly punches the boss on the shoulder with the palm of his hand. The boss flinches and blinks.

"Are you doing an estimate here?" The boss forces his lips into a smile but he sounds anything but happy. "I didn't think you had a dog …"

"No. No dog in the fight, so to speak." Sid says.

Dog fight? Have I missed something?

"But I keep tabs on opportunities for my students. Which reminds me. Have you thought about a little extra training for your dog here? If I recall, he was one of the ones with false alerts."

"One false alert. The only one he's had since I got him from Miguel." Now tension pours from the boss. I can see it in every line of his body. No wonder, when this guy can't keep his hands to himself. I watch to see if he tries to hit Josh again. Instead, he gives a little wave to the man behind the desk. "Can I steal Josh here for a second? Won't take long."

He takes Josh's arm and leads him back outside. Molly trails behind them halfway to the door and then stays behind as if unsure whether or not to follow. The glass doors close, but, once again my superior hearing comes through.

"Hey, I just wanted to let you know it's not too late to sign Doodle up for my class," Sid says, his arm still on the boss. "Our dogs have a pass-rate that's much higher than those who haven't had the class. And I think after his performance the other day, well—it's possible you're giving away the locations of the vials during practice."

"Doodle's doing fine."

Uh-oh. Molly slips out her camera and starts snapping photos of the boss and Sid. I hope neither of them notice.

"Well." Sid shrugs. "My experience is that these trials reflect what will happen on the test. Or worse. I've seen dogs that never missed a vial in practice fail the exam. It happens more than you'd think. My class bomb-proofs the dogs so they don't choke up on the big day. And it shows in the results."

The boss rubs his beard. "How much is it?"

"Normally, it's 3500 for a six week course. In your case, because there's only three weeks until the test, we'd have to do some private work, so it would be 3800."

"*Dollars*?" the boss asks. He shakes his head. "That's quite a racket."

Sid laughs, though his eyes flash briefly in a way that makes me even more alert. "Not a racket if you pass the test. You know as well as I do that with more and more pest control companies turning to bed bug dogs, the competition for work is increasing daily. Anyone with a NABBS certificate will have a distinct advantage over those who don't. Especially," Sid lowers his voice and I have to prick my ears to hear over the clicking of Molly's camera, "especially if the businesses find out that a company's dog failed the test. No apartment manager wants to spend money on a dog whose results might not be accurate."

"But aren't the NABBS results confidential?"

"Yes, but no one keeps *positive* results confidential. And I help my trainees out by providing certain hotels and apartment complexes with lists of those who have achieved their certifications. If you're not on the list … let's just say, if I were a manager, I'd work from the list."

"Are you threatening me?" The boss asks, his voice incredulous.

Sid smoothes his hair and laughs, shaking his head as if the boss said something crazy. But once again the hair on my back rises. "No threat, just giving you a way to increase the odds of success. Hey. Do what you like. But here's my card in case you change your mind. And remember, we only have three weeks, so if you do decide to take advantage of the training, you need to do it right away."

He shrugs into his jacket, then pulls out a card from an inside pocket. Molly's camera clicks again, then she pushes it out of sight just as Sid opens the door, leans inside and says, "See ya, Bill. Thanks again." With a wave and an oversized smile, he turns and leaves.

The boss is still holding the card when he comes back inside, grim faced and flushed.

I lie down beside Molly while we wait for the owner, who turns out to be an older woman dressed in a way that reminds me of Mrs. Franklin when she's going to church. This woman is thinner and older than Mrs. Franklin, but has the same no-nonsense attitude.

She and the boss talk for a while about what we'd charge to search the place for bed bugs. Then the boss has her hide some vials in one of the rooms and brings me in to find them. Piece of cake, as the boss often says. A curious expression, since, although cake is great—love it!—for a dog, at least, getting a piece is not always easy. And I've never found cake under a mattress or behind a dresser like I do the vials.

We all go back to the office. "So," the woman says, "has your dog there passed that NABBS test that Sid was talking about?"

"We take it in three weeks." He gives her a strained smile. "But he's been passing all the trials with flying colors."

Flying colors. Another phrase I just don't get. Birds have colors and they fly, but I don't think the boss is talking about birds. And airplanes are usually just one color—kind of gray ish, right? I remember when I was a pup, the first time a plane flew overhead, low and loud. Almost scared the water out of me. Anyway, can't for the life of me figure what any of this has to do with passing tests. I doze off.

Next thing I know Molly gives the leash a tug and we're headed back to the car.

Chapter 8

Dinner Guest

People love Fridays because the next day is the beginning of the weekend, which means they get to stay home from work. Or, in Molly's case, school. Which makes me a fan of weekends as well, even though I'm never quite sure when they're coming.

But today, the boss announces that this is Friday. The Friday that he invited Annie to come to dinner. So after Molly leaves for school, the boss spends the day vacuuming, mopping, dusting, and scrubbing because somehow, to hear him tell it, the house has to be "ready". For what, I'm not sure.

I stay out in the yard for most of this, which I'm happy to do even though I have to be on my chain. It's not that I'm *afraid* of vacuums—the service-dog people showed us they aren't dangerous—but they make a terrible roar that hurts my ears. And then there's the mop. That thing is just begging to be pounced on, but I've never met a boss who didn't get angry at a dog foolish enough to do so.

After school, Molly comes out to get me as usual. We're heading to her room when the boss emerges from the bathroom, his hands encased in funny-looking rubber gloves.

"Hey, Moll. Don't forget to clean your room."

"Why? Is she going to take a tour of the whole house?" From the angry way Molly spits this out, cleaning her room must be the last thing she wants to do. Can't say I blame her. A walk would be much more fun.

The boss seems to be taken aback, also. He stops, the surprise on his face giving way to a sad expression. "No," he says after a long silence. "I guess she doesn't have to see it."

Now Molly's face mirrors her father's, surprise followed by sadness. "Sorry," she mumbles. "I'll do it."

So Molly cleans her room while I nap on the fluffy rug by her bed.

Pretty soon the doorbell rings. Annie! I smell her before the door is open, and, if I'm not mistaken—yes!—Chloe is beside her.

"Doodle, calm *down*!" the boss says as he opens the door. He gives Annie a big smile, but I can smell that he's nervous. Whoa. Annie's nervous, too. What's with this?

The boss takes Annie's coat. "Glad to see you brought Chloe. Molly, why don't you take the dogs to the backyard where they can play. I don't think it's too cold, at least for awhile."

Great idea. I haven't had any real exercise all day. And I'm always up for a good game.

"Thanks, Molly," Annie says.

Molly takes Chloe's leash and heads for the back door. "Does Doodle have to be chained?"

"He'll be okay with another dog here."

Molly turns us loose outside. For such a little dog, Chloe turns out to be a fast runner. We play until we both collapse, panting, on the back porch. Then we each take long drinks. I have to say this is a *great* Friday.

Before long, Molly opens the door and calls us in. I can't help but drool at all the terrific smells in the kitchen. Annie, the boss and Molly all carry things to the dining room table, and then Molly and Annie take a seat. The boss lifts the foil from a wonderfully fragrant pan.

"Oh, lasagna! My favorite," Annie says.

He grins, clearly delighted. "Molly here will tell you that I'm no cook—" Molly nods in vigorous agreement—"but there's this little place off of Wilson Boulevard that makes great lasagnas. And garlic bread. But I *did* make the salad." He passes around a big bowl. "That's about the extent of my skills."

Annie takes a big helping of salad. "It all looks wonderful."

Smells even better. Both Chloe and I have small puddles of drool on the floor under our heads. All the good that'll do. I'm sure it'll be dry dog food as usual when we get *our* dinner. Which won't be until everyone at the table finishes. Even Molly doesn't give me food when she's at the table, so I ignore the growling in my stomach and take a nap.

When I awake, Annie's telling a story accompanied by hoots of laughter from the boss and Molly. All three of them are flushed and happy the way my second boss used to get after a few glasses of wine, but the only drinks on the table are water and sodas, including the boss's favorite, diet ginger ale. (Almost as bad as coffee. I had a few licks once when the boss spilled some on the floor.) I heard the boss tell someone—can't remember who now—that he had to give up wine and beer when "it started to become a problem." If the problem was anything like the way my second boss would act after a night's drinking, well then I'm glad he did.

The boss laughs so hard that he wipes his eyes with his napkin, and Molly seems more relaxed and happier than I've seen her in some time. And then, as I watch, I see her go still, as if she's suddenly remembering something, and the laugher drains from her face. She gives Annie an anxious, almost hostile glance.

"Dessert is just cookies, I'm afraid," the boss says, rising. He tilts his head toward Annie. "Coffee?"

"Sure," she says. "Cookies sound perfect."

My stomach rumbles in agreement.

"Hot chocolate, Molly?"

Molly shakes her head.

"Oh, and can you grab the plates?"

Without a word, Molly collects the plates and carries them to the kitchen. I follow her just in case she might want to scrape any remains into my dish. But she just sets them on the counter and returns to the dining table. I eye a crust of buttery bread on the edge of the top plate and reluctantly follow her.

I hear Annie say "Gunther" and perk up my ears.

"Jerry—now *there's* a piece of work," the boss exclaims. "I hope you hung up on him."

Annie takes a sip of coffee and smiles at him. "Mmm. Really good. I know, I know. Jerry has … issues. But he called to apologize, which he did profusely."

"Kicking dogs," the boss says darkly. "And the way he yelled at Molly. I'd like to give him some of his own medicine."

"I know. But I'm into *positive* reinforcement, remember?" Annie smiles at the boss. "Works with humans as well as dogs.

Jerry's … he seems a little bit desperate right now. And truly out of his depth with Gunther. Either he's the worst handler in the world—which is possible—or Gunther hasn't been properly trained."

The boss wipes a cookie crumb from his beard. "Or both. But I vote for the first. Who trained him?"

"A guy out of Maryland," Annie says with a little grimace. "Hosteler. I haven't heard of him. But Jerry said Sid recommended the trainer."

The boss lifts his eyebrows. "So that's why Sid acted less than thrilled to see him. He's trying to sell us thousands of dollars worth of training, and Gunther can't even find the vial."

It's Annie's turn to be surprised. "Thousands of dollars?"

The boss tells her about our encounter with Sid at the retirement home. "But maybe that's why he recommended this Hosteler. So he could charge Jerry to repair the damage. I wouldn't put it past him."

Annie shakes her head. "Unbelievable. Miguel doesn't think much of Sid as a trainer."

"I'm not sure I'd buy a hamburger on his say so, much less a twelve-thousand dollar dog," the boss agrees.

"True. But after talking with Jerry, I suspect two things are going on with Gunther. First, I think the trainer used harsh methods so Gunther has more fear than anticipation when he's doing a find." She looks at Molly. "I think those scabs you found on Gunther's neck might have come from the trainer, not Jerry."

Molly nods slightly, her eyes intent on Annie with such attention and yearning it reminds me of us dogs when we were working with Miguel, our eyes fixed on him hoping for praise or (in my case) some of his great treats.

Annie takes another sip from her cup and adds, "So, poor Gunther has a lot of anxiety going on. Sometimes, in these circumstances, when a dog is desperate to please someone, he'll alert even though he hasn't found the hide. Just to get the pressure off. But Gunther … I don't know. It's hard to tell how well he's been trained to even recognize the scent."

Molly nods again, that hungry expression still on her face as she watches Annie. Then, her face suddenly flushing, "I have video that might help. Of Gunther trying to find the vials."

"Really?" Annie's face lights up. "That'd be great." Then, frowning slightly, she says, "Wait. I thought you erased—?"

After another round of explanation, Molly says, "I wish we could get him away from Jerry. He wouldn't even let him have that treat. You can tell Gunther doesn't like him."

I'll say Poor Gunther. I know from experience that a dog with a bad boss is an unhappy dog.

"You're right, Molly. Gunther doesn't like him, and I think he's afraid of him," Annie says. "Most people wouldn't have noticed, but you're very good at reading dogs' body language. I bet you'd make a good trainer."

Molly beams at the compliment and then, for the second time tonight, catches herself and replaces the smile with a scowl.

The boss doesn't notice, mainly because for the whole evening his eyes have been pretty much set upon Annie.

"Speaking of handlers and dogs," he says, "I wonder if you'd have time to work with Doodle—see if he can still distinguish between live and dead bugs. Sid as good as told me that Doodle's success in the past is because I'm giving away the location of the vials with my body language."

Seriously? Wrong again.

"I don't think so," Annie says emphatically. "I've seen you work. But, sure, I'll be glad to run him through a few trials. Sunday afternoon?"

I doze off. After awhile, I wake up and they're *still* at the table talking. A dog could starve to death right before their eyes. I get up, shake, and move between Molly and the boss, giving them each a look that I hope will remind them that not everyone in the room has had dinner.

For once, it works, although Annie is the one who notices. She rises and picks up her cup. "I think the dogs are hungry. Should I feed them while you're clearing the dishes? I brought them a little treat."

Treats! How come I didn't smell that?

She digs down into her purse and comes up with two small cans. Ah, that explains it.

Annie pulls the lids off and I can't help but drool at the wonderful smell that wafts out. But what's that other scent? Anxiety pours off in waves from Annie. She clears her throat, and turns to Molly. "Maybe you'd like to come and help me test Doodle and Gunther. Before we all get together for the NABBS practice on Sunday. Your dad could drop you off and pick you up at my place when he comes for the practice."

Molly mumbles, "Maybe," and then almost runs out of the room, her face white as if Annie had said something to frighten her.

Annie sighs and stares at the cans of food. After a bit, Chloe touches a nose to her hand to remind her we *still* haven't eaten.

"Okay, okay," Annie says with a little laugh. And soon we're in the mudroom with our noses in our dishes. And, yes, we get the usual kibble, but it's topped with a few scrapings from the plates, including part of the buttery crust of bread *and* with the stuff from Annie's little cans. Delicious! I really like this Annie.

Molly, though—sometimes she acts like Annie's her favorite person in the world, and sometimes she seems to hate her. Or at least be anxious about her. For the life of me, I can't figure out why.

Chapter 9

Kenny

ANOTHER GREAT THING ABOUT FRIDAYS: THEY always seem to be followed by Saturdays. And today is going to be a great Saturday because the boss just dropped us off at the Franklin's. Tanya flings open the door, bubbling with excitement, and soon the girls are talking like greased lightning, an expression the boss uses to mean really fast, but one I frankly don't understand. I'm not afraid of lightning myself, but some poor dogs literally shake and sometimes even panic around lightning. Anyway, how anyone could grease lightning—let's just say the concept is beyond me.

As soon as we're in Tanya's bedroom with the door shut, Molly tells Tanya about Annie's visit. "My dad likes her," she says in a glum tone, as if this were a bad thing. I don't get it. We *all* like Annie, don't we? I remember those tasty little cans of dog food that she brought us and my mouth waters.

"Is she mean?" Tanya asks.

"No." Molly shakes her head. "Not mean at all. She's … nice. It's just that now that we found my mom …" She twists a piece of her hair, winding and unwinding it. "Dad says he and my mom will never get back together, but he hasn't even given it a chance, you know?"

"Does your mama know about her?" Tanya asks.

Another shake of the head. "No. They haven't seen each other since the day Doodle got shot."

Lots of excitement that day. I scratch the place the bullet hit. Still doing fine.

"Maybe if your mama knew about this Annie, she'd be jealous and come after your daddy."

Molly's eyes widen and she sucks in her breath. "Maybe. And I'm going to see her—my mom—in a few weeks. Unless..."

"So *maybe* you could just happen to *mention* Annie." They both smile in a strange way, as if they share a secret. I'm not sure what. But I know there's a lot Annie could teach Molly's mother about dogs. And, for that matter, about how to be nice to Molly.

After a while, we all go into the kitchen and Molly and Tanya make sandwiches. While I'm drooling over the smell of peanut butter, I hear a familiar slapping sound. Hey, Kenny's out in back practicing what he calls 'hoops.' I love Kenny. He calls me his best bud, and sometimes he throws a ball for me. Not a basketball, of course. I can say from experience that those things just weren't made to withstand a dog's teeth.

I stand with my nose to the door, hoping Molly will notice.

She doesn't, but Tanya does. "Can Doodle go out? Kenny's out there."

Molly considers it. "I guess it'll be okay. As long as the gate's shut."

The Franklins' backyard is mostly a big square of cement outlined by narrow bands of grass. Kenny stands near the basketball hoop, his skinny legs ending in big shoes that remind me of clowns.

I race over to him, and bow, inviting him to play. "Hey, Dude," he says in a depressed voice. He bounces the ball, up and down in a steady rhythm, not even stopping to give me a pat. He shoots, misses and says one of those words that the boss calls "language."

"Don't know why I bother. This boy won't be playing again."

His shoulders slump and he stares at his feet. Whoa. A drop splatters on the cement next to his foot. I glance up at the sky but realize it's not rain. It's a tear.

The door clicks open. Molly and Tanya come outside each holding a sandwich.

Kenny swipes his hand across his face, turning his back to the girls.

"Hey, Ken," Tanya says softly. "You okay?"

"Yeah." Kenny doesn't look at them.

"You want a sandwich? I'll make you one."

"I'm good."

Really? Because he sounds anything *but* good. In fact, I've never heard him sound this way—angry and sad all mixed together.

"I know you didn't do it," Molly says.

Tanya adds, "Yeah. It was that Justin Everly, wasn't it? Mama says his family's always been on the trashy side of tracks."

Kenny doesn't answer. He stands up and starts bouncing the ball again, still not looking at the girls. Maybe because, like me, he's not sure what they're talking about. But I must be wrong, because then he speaks in a tight, low voice.

"Even if Justin had my combination—speaking *hypothetically,* right?—I can't do nothin' 'bout it. Because if I tell that cop 'bout Justin, everybody'll just say I did it to save my own skin. And even if it's true, I'll still be a—" he uses another language word here—"snitch, and to all my friends that's way worse than smoking pot."

"Even at Tri-State?" Molly asks. "I mean it's supposed to be a good school."

Kenny shakes his head. "That's what Mama don't understand. She thinks 'cause Arlington has this reputation, that everything's different there." He stops and holds the ball. "And it's a good school, good teachers and all. But some things are the same no matter where you go. Coach Thatcher good as told me that if I talked to the cops, I'd lose all respect from the team."

"But that's not fair!" Molly tosses me the crust to her sandwich. I take the time to eat it carefully, since the boss isn't around to notice. "He's says you're supposed to drop out of school for something you didn't do just so everyone'll *respect* you? Wreck your whole future?"

"He didn't say those exact words, but that's what he meant. And I don't want to be no snitch, but I don't want to quit the team, and school and . . ." Kenny's voice breaks. He thrusts the ball up and down in hard, fast strokes.

"You gotta tell them," Tanya says, sounding near tears herself.

"Tell them what?" Kenny says, his voice firm again. "I said *hypothetical.* Don't you tell this to no one."

Both Molly and Tanya start to object, but Kenny interrupts. "No one. You hear?"

Reluctant nods from both girls. Tanya sighs. Kenny keeps bouncing the ball in a steady pattern. Molly squints at the ground the way she does sometimes when she's thinking hard about something. Then she looks up.

"What if we could find a way to prove Justin did it without you saying anything?"

Kenny's mouth tightens in a grimace. "How you gonna do that?"

"I don't know," Molly says. "But maybe..." she turns to me and rests a hand on my back. "Maybe we can figure out a way."

The ball hits the ground with extra force and makes a loud slap when Kenny catches it. "Right. Let me know when you do."

Molly stiffens at that, but then she says, "Come on, Doodle." She goes to the door and back into the kitchen, Tanya and me at her heels.

Mrs. Franklin glances up from a cutting board where she's chopping some green peppers. Not too fond of them myself, but I can eat them if there's nothing better around. I search the floor just in case any bits might have fallen from the counter. No luck.

"Kenny doing okay?" She says this in a flat voice, as if she already knows the answer and doesn't like it.

Tanya nods, and hurries through the kitchen. Molly and I rush to keep up. As soon as we're in Tanya's bedroom, Tanya shuts the door and leans her back against it.

"That was close. I don't want Mama askin' me what Kenny said. I don't want to be tellin' her lies." She sighs and plops down on the bed. "Now, what's this about catching Justin?"

Molly sits beside her. "Like we talked about before. If we could train Doodle to alert on pot, we could take him to school, and maybe if he did an alert on Justin, the cops would know he's the one."

"You gonna just call the cops and ask them to go to school with you and Doodle?" She rolls her eyes. "Yeah, that'll work. They love taking orders from kids."

"But if I told them I knew who was really guilty …" Molly rolls a section of her hair between her fingers, twisting and untwisting it.

"Dream on, girl."

For a moment, they both sit in a glum silence. I'm thinking this might be a good time for a nap. And then Tanya straightens and says, "Unless…"

"Unless what?"

"Unless the cop was your mom. She'd come if you ask, right?"

Molly's lips stretch into a tight line. She clutches the end of her hair, her hand still. "Maybe," she says, at last. "I'm not sure. She didn't come to career day."

"But this is different. She could solve a case. Maybe get a promotion."

"Maybe." Molly frowns. She starts twisting the hair again, rapidly. "But what if I call her and she doesn't come?" She looks suddenly as forlorn as a dog stuck on a chain in the backyard. "What then?"

Chapter 10

Gunther Fails a Test

TODAY, IT'S SUNDAY, WHICH IS ANOTHER GREAT DAY IN the week although, frankly, I can't keep quite keep them all straight. We're on the way to Miguel's so I can work with Annie. And the good news is that Molly decided she'd go. "So I'll know how to train you and we can clear Kenny," she told me, right before she called Annie to say she'd be coming. Not sure exactly what she means, but I'm always glad to have her come along.

According to the boss, it takes forty-five minutes to get to Miguel's place, which is out of the city.

"Isn't this great?" he says, as the van bumps along Miguel's driveway. "Wish we could afford to live out here."

Miguel lives in a little white house next to what he calls his barn—a large metal building that has a training area in the center and kennels along the sides and in the back. The kennels open up to narrow, fenced dog runs that all have gates to this really great field. "Three acres," Miguel used to say when he'd open the gates and let a few of us out at a time to stretch our legs. "Go for it."

Beyond that is an even bigger fenced pasture, where he keeps two horses. Miguel never lets any dogs into that field, which is fine by me. Got kicked by a horse once, about which I'll simply say, Not Fun. Who'd have thought a little barking in an effort to get a friendly game of chase going would make a horse so upset? Unpredictable creatures, all of them, and now I keep my distance.

But I'd love to have a romp in the dog field. I bet there are lots of scents out there to catch up on. Lots of new dogs. Maybe a few squirrels. Maybe—

"Doodle, hush!" the boss says, turning off the engine.

Oh. Guess I got a little excited.

As soon as the boss lets me out of the van, I'm breathing in all the familiar scents—Miguel's, of course, and Annie's—and all the glorious country smells. Grass, weeds, trees, leaves, dirt, dog poop, horse manure, rusting metal from Miguel's trash pile behind the barn. I can hardly take it all in.

Annie hurries from the barn, a fat bunch of keys jangling from her belt. Hey, those are Miguel's keys. I know the sound well. I remember the days us dogs would lie in our kennels and listen for the thud of his footsteps and the jingling of his keys. It always meant something good when Miguel came to get us.

I raise my nose and sniff, hoping we'll get to see him. His pockets *always* have treats. But his scent, while everywhere, isn't fresh. Which is why I'm not surprised by Annie's answer when the boss asks if Miguel is home.

"He's in Florida right now at a seminar for scent-detection trainers, and then he's visiting his sister's family. Gets back on Thursday."

"Oh." The boss seems almost as disappointed as I am, though, to my knowledge, Miguel never gives *him* treats.

"Ready, Molly?" Annie asks.

Speaking of horses, Molly seems as skittish as a mare on a windy day. "Yeah," she answers in a voice several tones higher than normal. I'm not sure either the boss or Annie notices, not just because humans tend to be clueless about such things, but also because whenever the boss and Annie are together, they don't seem to notice much at all.

The boss opens the door to the van, but hesitates. "So, your place at three?" Annie nods. "Don't worry. I'll take good care of them. Enjoy your movie."

With that, the boss, looking like he'd much rather stay, gets in and drives off.

"I guess we'd better get to work," Annie says.

She puts us in what she calls the observation area, which is several rows of folding chairs lined up facing some sets of furniture. Molly sits in one of the front chairs, and begins twisting the ends of her hair. I lie down in front of her and sample the scents of the dogs coming from the kennels. None that I've met, but then Miguel always was good at finding new bosses for his trainees.

We're facing three rooms divided by short walls no taller than my head, connected by doorways leading from one room to the other. I've heard Miguel tell his clients that these are meant to look like rooms in an apartment or home. Two of the rooms have beds and dressers and something Miguel calls armoires. Never heard the word before coming here, and, frankly, I've never seen one in a real home, but I gather they're a type of fake closet. The other room has several couches as well as some end tables with lamps. I found a vial in one of the lampshades once. Miguel was quite proud of me.

"Let's run Doodle through first," Annie says. She takes the leash and leads me into the area with the furniture.

"Find," she commands. I sniff my way around the first room, taking care to check the places where I've found vials before. Nothing there, so I make my way into the next one. Aha! I find a vial taped to the underside of a couch, and one in the floor of the closet. Annie, grinning broadly, pays me for each find with her delicious treats. I ignore the vial of dead bugs under the mattress in that room and the one in the sofa cushion in the last room as well.

"Perfect!" Annie says, giving me several treats. "He didn't alert on the dead ones."

From her chair, Molly claps and says "*Good* dog. I still don't think he made a mistake last week. I think Sid—I don't know—I think he did something."

Annie says, "Well, even the best dogs can give false alerts sometimes. We don't know what they're smelling—maybe there was something that interfered with the scent. Or that scent was there from a previous exposure. But the good news is that he's alerting on accurate finds without any problem."

Annie walks me over to Molly, who gives me some treats also. This is what I like about bed bug work.

Annie goes to the back and returns a few minutes later with Gunther on a leash. I can see in a flash that he likes Annie better than Jerry. His head is higher, as is his tail, although his tail is still at a height that indicates caution. He glances at us, gives a sniff in our direction, and then turns his attention back to Annie.

She leads Gunther to the living room and gives the "find" command. He starts casting about.

Gunther sniffs and sniffs, but in the way of a dog searching for any trace of the scent, not one who has caught the trail and is circling closer. His sniffing is interrupted by fleeting, anxious looks at Annie, as if he's worried she might be angry. Or perhaps he hopes she'll show him where to look. I remember suddenly how Jerry would shift his weight when Gunther got close to a vial. Fat chance of that with Annie. If she's anything like Miguel, she's way too smart to give Gunther any clues.

At any rate, it's obvious Gunther isn't close to anything yet. Maybe he should try the sofa in the next room. I found a vial there, once.

Annie turns and smiles at Molly. "So far, so good on the scent detecting. There weren't any vials in this room. But something in Gunther's behavior worries me. Can you see what it is?"

"The way he keeps looking at you? He almost seems scared."

"Excellent observation. I really think you might have the instincts to be a good dog trainer."

Molly flushes at this, and drops her hand from her hair.

"Gunther seems more concerned by my *reactions* to his search than about the search itself. I saw the same behavior in the video you sent me of our practice last week. This can come from using negative reinforcement—something the dog doesn't like, like a harsh collar correction—rather than positive reinforcement, which would be to give him treats or a favorite toy when he gets it right. In more timid animals like Gunther, negative reinforcement can increase his anxiety to the point that it interferes with his learning."

"Plus it makes him feel bad," Molly says."Where giving him treats wouldn't." Her hands are now relaxed on her lap.

I have to agree. Treats *never* make me feel bad.

"Exactly." Annie nods approvingly. "Gunther's worrying more about what I'll do if he doesn't find the bed bugs than about actually *finding* them. But we still need to see if he can even find the bugs at all. So let's try the next room and see what happens."

She leads Gunther into one of the fake bedrooms and gives the command. Just as before, Gunther casts about for a scent. I'm afraid he's not going to find anything all. But then he circles his way in to one corner of the mattress, pauses, then looks up at Annie. She stands like a statue. Gunther starts panting, which tells me he's anxious because it's plenty cool here in the barn. Finally, he gives the alert.

Annie sighs, lifts the mattress and removes a vial.

"Dead ones?" Molly asks.

"Yep. As I suspected. He hasn't been well-trained."

Gunther watches her, drooling a little, clearly hoping for a reward. Annie hesitates then gives him a treat and then kneels down and strokes him gently under his chin. "I don't want him to get discouraged," she says, "and I want training to be a positive experience, so I'm rewarding him anyway. If I were going to pursue his training, what I'd do is go back to square one and teach him to alert only on live bed bugs."

"Aren't you going to do it? Train him, I mean?"

Annie, still stroking Gunther, doesn't look up. "He's not my dog," she says softly. "And Miguel is running a business, not a charity. We could train him if Jerry hired us, but I doubt Jerry wants to pay for more training. Which is too bad because Gunther is not a good bed bug dog at this point."

"What about the practice this afternoon?" Molly's voice takes on tones of alarm. "If Gunther fails again, Jer—um, Mr. Alben—might take it out on him." Her fingers move back up to her hair and start twisting. "You saw his neck."

Annie's lips tighten into a straight line. "Yeah, I'm worried about that—Jerry getting angry. Although I don't think the scars on his neck came from Jerry. He's only had Gunther for about ten days, and they look older than that."

She massages Gunther's neck. When she stops, he licks her hand then noses it for her to continue.

"What if..." I hear Molly swallow and, whoa, now I can smell her tension. "What if you taught me how to do it? How to train a dog to know one scent from another. We could do it when you're not working, so Miguel wouldn't get mad—and we could use Gunther as the dog."

Annie turns to her. "You'd really like to learn?" She sounds quite happy at the prospect.

"Yeah." Molly's face flushes and she twirls an end of hair. "I'd really like to."

"I don't know how long Jerry would let me keep Gunther..." Annie scratches behind one of his ears and Gunther gazes up at her as if he's found the love of his life.

Suddenly, a strident buzzing makes all four of us jump. Annie pulls her phone from her jeans' pocket and flips it open. "Annie Harmon."

Even with my excellent hearing, I can't quite extract the words from the squawking coming through the earpiece. I recognize the voice, though, and so does Gunther, who suddenly starts scratching behind his ear.

"Oh. Hi, Jerry." Annie raises her eyebrows at Molly. "We were just talking about you. We ran Gunther through some trials today and I wanted to talk—"

More squawking. Annie listens, eyes widening. "Sounds awful," she says when the squawking stops. "You're wise not to leave the house. And everyone will be glad you're not sharing it with them."

A short pause. "No problem. In fact, I was going to ask if I might keep Gunther for a few extra days and work with him. He's not distinguishing between live and dead bed bugs, and I wanted—"

Another explosion of sound. Annie moves it away from her ear. This time I catch a few words. "Money back" and "only three weeks now."

"I know." Pause. "Yes, I know." Annie speaks in a soothing voice, as if she's trying to calm a nervous dog. "We can work with him. And no problem. Just get well and we'll talk about it. I think we can turn him around."

Finally, she snaps her phone shut. "Well," she says, breaking into a smile. "We won't have to worry about how Gunther will do today. Jerry has stomach flu and won't be coming to practice."

"That gives us time. We could do the training." Molly's eyes have the same expression as a dog begging for treats.

"We can start it. I don't know how far we'll get in just a few days..." She strokes Gunther's head. "But maybe if we make progress, Jerry will let me keep him longer. If I told him I was retraining him for free, he *might* go for it." She stares, eyes unfocused for a minute, then stands up. "Okay. Let's do it! Lesson one coming right up. We'll just have to hope that Jerry will let us keep going long enough to make a difference."

Pretty soon Annie has set up a course and she and Molly are working with Gunther. Can't say I'm all that interested. Been there, done that, as my first boss used to say, and nothing Gunther does is going to get me a treat. I doze off.

Next thing I know, Molly's tugging at the leash. "Let's go," she says.

She loads me into a crate in Annie's van, which looks a lot like the boss's but has many more interesting dog smells, and soon we're on the road.

Molly asks questions about training during the ride back while I mostly nap, as riding in cars makes me sleepy. So it hardly seems any time before Annie is pulling up into her garage. Molly releases me in the backyard where I greet Chloe and then hurry over to the fence to relieve myself. Chloe and I play a great game of chase until we hear the boss's van pull up in the driveway.

He comes through the gate carrying a fragrant dish—some kind of chicken that smells really wonder—

"Doodle, *off*," he says.

Oh. I follow him to the patio door hoping I might get a taste of the chicken, but, as usual, he takes it into the kitchen. Molly clicks a leash on my collar and then takes her camera out from the pocket of her windbreaker and snaps a few photos.

People and dogs keep arriving until we have the usual group together—Orlando and the horsey-faced woman with their beagles, the smoker-man with his Labrador and others that I don't know as well. I exchange greetings with the dogs, their scents telling me where they've been. All the humans bring some kind of food and pretty soon the smells coming from Annie's kitchen are making us dogs drool. For all the good it'll do. As usual, the people will keep it all for themselves. Good thing I can smell treats in all the bosses' pockets. Otherwise a dog could get discouraged.

Pretty soon, we're all taking turns finding bed bugs. When I'm up, I find all my vials without problem.

"Perfect!" the boss says, sounding more relieved than happy. "No false alerts."

Annie smiles. "And none earlier today. So relax. You have nothing to worry about. Whatever happened to Doodle last week isn't becoming a pattern."

"Whatever happened last week wasn't Doodle's fault," Molly says with conviction. "We have to trust his nose."

Couldn't have said it better myself.

Chapter 11

Complications

According to the boss, we're having a busy week. I'm not sure what he means by "we" since our only job turns out to be a small one at a nursing home in Alexandria. Not Waddell, which has never called him back. I heard the boss tell Annie that he thinks Sid might have lost us the job. So I'm mostly lying around the house, which isn't what I'd call busy.

The boss, though, spends a lot of time cleaning his rifles and stuffing things into an enormous backpack with metal edges.

"Deer season opens this weekend," he says, in one of his now frequent phone calls to Annie. "Matt—he's my brother—and I always go. It's become a tradition."

Deer season. I lift my ears. Chased a lot of deer in my puppy days. Kind of a tradition for us dogs, too. And when the bosses shot a deer, they'd sometimes leave the carcass in the gully down behind the barn. Lots of good eating on a carcass, not to mention a great supply of bones to chew on.

"—watch Doodle," the boss is saying. "I don't want him anywhere near gunfire. *That's* an accident waiting to happen, if you know what I mean."

Annie's laughter comes through the phone. Don't know why. All I can say about the time I got shot? Not my fault. I scratch at the place the bullet grazed me where, as Mrs. Franklin puts it, I took a bullet for Molly. Still fine. Then the boss tells Annie all about Matt, how he owns a small heating and cooling company in Alexandria, has two kids, and how his wife teaches piano.

"He's the reason I decided to start my business here." They talk some more and then I hear Annie ask something about Molly.

"Thanks, but she's going to stay with her mother." He sighs and strokes his beard. "I'm not thrilled, but she's determined to do it. I just hope she doesn't worry herself to death before she goes."

He's right about Molly and worrying. When she gets home from school, she's as busy as the boss with her packing. She opens a small suitcase on her bed and puts a box in it.

"Scrabble," she says. I tilt my head trying to understand. "Dad says that he and Mom used to play it all the time and that she was really good. So maybe we can play—have a game night. Families get closer when they play games together. Everyone knows that."

Oh. Games. Never heard of Scrabble, but if it involves a ball or any kind of chasing, count me in.

"Popcorn!" She rushes to the kitchen and pulls a couple of salty-smelling packages from a cupboard, puts them in a plastic bag and drops it into the suitcase. "Oh, and maybe—" she goes back into the kitchen and gets a big bag of chocolate almonds. Delicious. I know because I've grabbed a few fallen ones. Don't get me started on how humans never give us dogs anything with chocolate.

Clothes come next. Molly packs some, frowns at her suitcase, takes them out and exchanges them for different ones. Then she takes those out and dresses in them, staring at herself in the mirror that hangs on the inside door of her closet.

"What do you think, Doodle?" she asks me more than once.

I tell her what I think, but Molly, who normally understands my let's-go-for-a-walk body language, seems unusually clueless.

This goes on for several days: the boss getting all his equipment together, Molly packing and unpacking, me lying around wishing for a walk. Every night, before climbing into bed, Molly makes a mark on her calendar. And then one night she says, "Tomorrow, Doodle. I'm scared."

She smells scared when she gets home from school the next day. She's zipping up her suitcase after yet again changing some of the contents, when the boss's phone rings.

"Oh, no," she whispers. "She's going to cancel." She hurries out to the living room.

But when the boss glances down at his phone, his face spreads into a big smile. He never looks like that talking to Molly's mother. And then he says, "Hi, Annie. What's up?"

Molly gives a little sigh of relief.

Annie's voice comes over the phone, thick and hoarse. "I'm so sorry. I think I've come down with that flu that's going around. I feel awful. I can hardly walk from my bed to the bathroom. I don't see how I can take Doodle. My sister's coming over to get Chloe and keep her for the weekend." She coughs, clears her throat, then coughs some more. "I hate doing this to you. I hope this doesn't ruin your trip."

The boss frowns, his face drooping in disappointment, but when he speaks, his voice has the false cheerfulness he sometimes uses with Molly. "Oh, no, Annie. Don't worry about it.

Can I pick up anything? Some chicken soup from Soup N' Stuff?"

"No, I'm okay. My sister's bringing some food and juice. I just feel terrible that I can't take Doodle. Maybe Miguel has room for him."

"Good idea. Matt and I will be going in that direction anyway."

As soon as he's off the phone with Annie, the boss tries Miguel.

"Sorry," Miguel says, after the boss has explained the situation. "I came back with three rescues from the county shelter in Florida and I don't have empty space."

"Hey, no problem," the boss says, still using that fake cheerful voice. But when he snaps his phone shut, he slumps down into a chair and mutters a few words of "language" under his breath.

Molly watches him for a minute. "Maybe I could take Doodle with me," she says. "We could ask my mom."

The boss grimaces. "I don't want to ask Cori. A lot of people don't like dogs in their homes."

Something I don't understand at all. Just sayin'.

"I'll call her," Molly says. She throws her arms around my neck. "Then, I'll have a friend with me. In case … in case I need it."

As usual, the boss can't resist Molly. But he insists on making the call. From the conversation, I gather that Molly's mom is reluctant at first—again, no idea why. I haven't chewed furniture or had what humans like to call an "accident" since I was a puppy.

"He's well-trained. He was a service dog for a while."

A very *short* while, but fortunately he doesn't go into that.

Cori finally agrees. Just like that, the boss is cheerful again, and even Molly seems less nervous. They load my spare crate into the van—my other one stays in the van—along with my food, my leash and harness, my stakeout chain, some of my toys—"It's like taking an infant—" the boss complains at one point. And soon we're all rolling down the highway.

"Don't let Doodle outside by himself unless he's chained up," the boss says. "You know how he is with fences. And don't walk him without the pinch collar. He's too powerful—"

Molly's phone rings. "Hey," she says.

I can't hear who it is through the noise of the engine.

"Oh, no!" Molly says. "Oh, *no!* How can they do that?"

The boss gives Molly a worried glance. "Who is it? Cori? Is she canceling?"

"Tanya," Molly whispers with her hand over the mouthpiece. Then, back into the phone, "Did they get a lawyer?"

The boss begins to rap his fingers on the steering wheel.

"Oh, I'm so sorry." Molly says this several more time until finally she says, "Yeah, my mom's. I'll call you," and clicks her phone shut.

"What happened?"

"They arrested Kenny. The police said they plan to press charges. They want to make an example of him."

"His poor parents," the boss sighs, his fingers rapping away.

"Poor *Kenny.* I know he didn't do it. He practically *told* us that it was Justin Everly, but he said his coach told him no one likes a snitch."

"That's an odd thing to say. You'd think his coach would encourage him to tell the truth. Especially with so much at stake."

"Tanya says her brother thinks it's cause Kenny's black and Justin's white and black people always get accused of being druggies."

"Which brother? Derrin?"

Molly nods.

"I don't know that anyone would have that attitude at that school. But the cops—I wouldn't be surprised. Wish there was something we could do." The boss's fingers beat steadily on the wheel.

"Yeah. Maybe we could—" Molly glances at me and then looks back at her dad. Whoa. Anxiety suddenly pours off her.

"We could what?" He cranes his head as we pass through a light, his voice distracted.

Molly twists the ends of her hair, and takes a deep breath. "Well, we could use Doo—"

The boss interrupts. "Is this 29th? Can you read the sign?"

Molly swallows and then peers out the window. "30th."

The boss makes a sudden turn. Good thing my crate is bolted down or I'd be against the window. "I swear if they made the street names any smaller they'd be invisible."

He makes several more turns, then says, "Sorry. What were you saying?"

"Nothing." Molly alternately twists and chews on the ends of her hair. She doesn't speak again until the boss pulls over to the curb, turns off the engine, and says in a strained voice, "Well, here we are."

We're parked in front of a small white house that sits in an extremely narrow yard. On either side and all down the street are similar small houses in tiny yards. Only a few of the homes have trees. Not a paradise for dogs. I can see that right away.

I'm glad I saw Molly pack the scooper because otherwise that tiny yard could quickly become intolerable.

Molly attaches the leash and takes me out of the crate while the boss grabs an armful of the stuff we brought. I sample the air. Other than the nervous tension pouring from both the boss and Molly, I smell nothing unusual—musty leaf mold, the acrid scent of gas and oil on the asphalt, grass, smoke from a chimney down the block, barbecue smoke from a place the opposite direction, a variety of human scents, several dogs, and the inevitable cats.

An uneven strip of concrete, shot through with cracks and with weeds poking through the cracks leads to the front porch. Cori opens the door before we reach the steps. She looks the same as the last time I saw her—slender, skin the same color brown as Miguel's, dark straight hair that doesn't quite reach her shoulders. She smells the same, too, except today I don't detect the metallic smell of a gun under her clothing.

"You made it," she says, as nervous as Molly and the boss by the sound of it. "Hi, Doodle." I wag my tail in response . But then, a scent coming from the house distracts me. Bad news, right off. One of those cats I smelled when I got out of the van must live here. Female. I sniff some more. Food, like the kind the boss gets at his favorite Mexican restaurant. And another human: a woman.

The boss hauls several loads from the van, ending with my portable crate, which collapses into something easy to carry. "Would you like me to carry this in? Help set it up?"

"We can do it," Cori says, moving in front of the open door as if to block his passage.

The boss, usually oblivious to body language, doesn't miss this. "Okay. Good." He rubs his beard, shifts his weight from one foot to the other, then pulls out a paper from inside his coat and thrusts it at Cori. “Here’s all the emergency information. I’ll have my cell, but if you can’t get me, Matt’s wife, Jenny, will be home all weekend. “You remember Matt?—”

Cori nods. “Of course.” Her tone makes it sound as if the question was beyond stupid. “Don’t worry, we’ll be fine.”

From the scent of her nervous sweat, she’s not as sure about that as she sounds. All this emotion is getting to me. I suppress a whine and scratch an ear. But smells are invisible to the boss. He heaves a sigh of relief. “Okay. Good.” He bends to give Molly a stiff hug, then nods at Cori. “Thanks again. I’ll be back Sunday afternoon.”

Cori and Molly watch from the porch until the van turns the corner at the end of the street.

“Well,” Cori says, “I guess we’d better go in.”

Chapter 12

The Visit

I'M ON HIGH ALERT AS MOLLY LEADS ME THROUGH THE door because cats are the very essence of unpredictability. Worse than horses, frankly, although not as dangerous. Even though I know how to behave when walking into a strange home, I can't guarantee that this cat might not spring at me from some corner of the room. Especially since, technically, I'm invading her territory. Forewarned is forearmed, as Miguel used to say, although he usually was talking about how he approached aggressive dogs.

I'm not the only one on high alert. Molly's anxiety travels down the leash, not to mention that I can smell it on her and hear her heart thumping away. I'm not sure if she's worried about the cat, too, or about something else.

My nails click on the wood floor, shiny and reeking of wax. Despite all my service dog training, shiny floors still make me the teensiest bit nervous. But I hold my head high, watchful for any sudden movement.

"I have someone eager to meet you," Cori says, "in the living room." She motions us through a doorway to where a woman, her gray hair pulled back into a knot behind her head, sits in a stuffed chair. A whole cluster of scents come from her: garlic, onion, furniture polish and wax, very faint traces of incense (learned about that when we went into certain churches during my service dog training), and a musty scent of old clothes or furniture.

When she sees us, the woman's face creases into a giant smile. She drops the book on a little table by the chair and rises, a little stiffly, regarding us with alert but friendly black eyes. She's wearing jeans and a bright yellow shirt, and thick-soled white shoes.

"María," she says, infusing the word with joy and longing.

For a second, I'm confused, but then I remember that María is Molly's first name. María Maureen Hunter, as she's told me more than once, always adding that she's named after her two grandmothers. Don't know why humans have so many names. Doodle, while not the name I would have chosen for myself, does fine for me all by itself.

Cori says something in Spanish, and the old woman answers back in a low, scratchy voice. I learned a little Spanish in my service dog days, and then some more with Miguel, but I can't say that I'm able to follow the conversation. I can't tell if Molly does or not—she loves Spanish and is always practicing it with this disembodied scentless nasal voice that comes from her computer, so maybe. She stands still, eyes wide, listening.

Cori says in English, "Molly, this is my aunt—your *great* aunt—Señora Benita Flores." She hesitates, then points to Molly and says to the woman "Benita … *M'ija* … my daughter, María."

The woman reaches out and takes Molly's hand in her own gnarled one. "María, María. Last time I saw you was at your baptism. You weighed less than seven pounds!" She squeezes Molly's hands with both of hers. "*Chica, chica.* You've grown into a beautiful girl. Oh, I wish your nana could be here to see you."

Molly flushes at this. "Nice to meet you," she murmurs. Then, lowering her eyes, "Everyone calls me Molly now."

Benita pats her hand and then releases it. "Molly, then. But in here—" she presses a fist to her breast "—in here you'll always be María."

Molly, turning to her mother, asks, "Is she the one..." she grabs an end of her hair and looks at her feet. "Was it her house you went to when...?"

"Yes," Cori says, clipping the word short.

Benita says something in Spanish and this time Molly answers in that language, flushing even more deeply. Benita laughs with pleasure. "And you speak Spanish, too."

Molly flushes. "A little," she says. "I'm still learning."

I see a flash of motion behind the couch. I crinkle my nose in that direction.

Definitely the cat. I scoot toward it as far as the leash will allow. Ah, there she is. Peeking around the leg of the couch, watching me, her scent now strong in my nose. But I don't smell fear. Her body language gives no sign of it either, nor of that hissing, spitting anger that cats are so often inclined toward. Interesting. She's one self-possessed cat. She stares at me until I have to look away and scratch an ear.

And then, to my astonishment, as if a dog—a *big* dog—weren't sitting right in front of her, the cat saunters out and begins to rub against Molly's jeans.

"Oh, a calico," Molly says with (in my opinion) entirely unjustified enthusiasm. She bends over and strokes the cat. I should do something about this—really I should—but somehow all I can do is watch.

Benita laughs with delight. "That's Miga. Because she's been *mi amiga* ever since she showed up at the door as a kitten, half-starved and yowling."

Molly picks her up. "Nice to meet you, Miga. You're beautiful." She turns back to Benita. "How old is she?"

I bump my nose against Molly's arm to remind her that I haven't been introduced yet. But she keeps going on about the cat, with no sign of noticing.

Benita frowns at Cori. "Do you remember how old she was when you came?"

Cori reaches over and strokes the cat's head. "She was three."

"Three," Molly says with an odd catch in her voice. "The same age as I was when—" she stops, the flush in her face deepening. Her heartbeat, which had slowed down some, speeds up again.

"So. You two are about the same age." Cori says in a quick, eager-to-move-on voice. "Now, about dinner. Benita has prepared a special meal in your honor."

Dinner always sounds good to me, but Molly's still holding the cat. And I still haven't been introduced. I bump her again."

"Why Doodle, you're jealous," Molly says with a laugh.

I don't think wishing for a little acknowledgement qualifies as jealousy.

Benita bends over and pats me on the head with a stiff hand. I try not to shrink away. "So you're the famous Doodle, the fearless dog. I didn't realize you'd be so big."

I *am* big. Something that cat ought to keep in mind.

But if fearless describes anyone in the room, it's this cat, Miga. Molly sets her down and she strolls calmly over to me. I try to stare her down, but somehow end up averting my eyes, and the next thing I know Miga begins to twine herself around *my* legs.

"Look at that," Molly exclaims. "Doodle has a new friend."

Hah. That's putting it *way* too strongly. I step away from her.

Molly and I follow Cori and Benita into the kitchen, a big window-lit room with a round table at one end. On the backside of the room, next to the fridge, is a door that leads outside. Miga races in, startling me, and runs over to a dish of water and another dish of kibble by the door. Probably cat food, which I like just fine despite the name, but I can't tell because all the delicious smells from the stove overwhelm my nose.

"Nice, no?" Benita says. "The kitchen used to be small, hardly big enough to hold the ants. We had it redone a few years ago when I retired."

I start to drool.

Cori bends her head toward me. "Does he need to go outside? The backyard is fenced."

"He's fine inside. He's doesn't beg or anything."

I'll say not. Especially since it never gets me anywhere.

They all carry steaming dishes to the table. The food, according to Molly's exclamations, consists of the best enchiladas and chili rellenos she's ever had. Naturally, I wouldn't know, but it smells good.

I've always liked Mexican food, which I used to get from my second boss who'd buy it in these Styrofoam containers (Styrofoam—now that's a weird substance. I don't recommend eating it.) He never finished the food himself, preferring his beer and what he called "his friend," Jim Beam, which, oddly, was not a person but a bottle of whiskey. (Vile stuff.) So he'd eat a little and then lose interest, and I'd finish it off while he slept on the couch. Good thing, too, as more often than not, he'd forget to give me my kibble. There's not much I want to remember from that boss, but I did learn to like all sorts of food he called "take out."

Dinner lasts a long time. I don't understand why humans like to take forever to eat. Well, actually I do. It's because they eat a bite, talk, talk some more, eat another bite, talk and talk some more. Really, if they'd just keep quiet and focus they could get through a meal in a reasonable amount of time. Look at us dogs. We don't take a bite, bark, bark some more, then take another bite. We get the job done. (Unless there's an intruder, of course, or some threat. But that's different.) They could learn from our example.

At first, this isn't the case. After all the usual compliments about the food, they eat in silence. Molly casts nervous glances at her mother, who in turn asks a few polite questions that Molly answers just as politely. Everyone seems on guard. But that's good for me as it means they'll get through dinner more quickly.

But just as I'm getting my hopes up, Cori says, "Benita is the first person in our family to become a naturalized citizen."

"Except you," Molly says, then catches herself. "Oh, but you were born here."

"That's right. I'm a citizen by birth. But Benita didn't have it so easy. When she and my mother were children, they were too poor to afford any education, which was very expensive in Mexico. But one of her aunts worked as a cook for a priest, and this aunt adopted Benita and raised her, so that Benita could go to the local parochial school."

Benita smiles and wipes the corner of her mouth with her napkin. "She taught me to cook, too." She tilts her head toward the platter of food that is still making my mouth water.

Cori talks some more about how hard Benita worked, first to get her education and then to become a citizen, and how without the help from her aunt and that priest, Benita would have never left Mexico. I doze off, dreaming briefly about enchiladas, only to wake up to another pause in the conversation. I raise my head, hoping that at last they're done. No luck.

Benita asks Molly about her interest in photography. This is a subject Molly can't resist—she often expounds at length to me about some aspect of her camera that, frankly, goes right over my head. It's as if I tried to explain to her all the different scents on a single blade of grass.

And from there, the conversation moves to me and my job. Molly can't resist launching into story after story about our bed bug exploits. She tells them how Miguel found me in an animal shelter the day before I was going to be euthanized—still don't know what that means but gather it's bad—and trained me to be a bed bug dog. And how she and the boss came to Miguel's looking to get a beagle, but how she knew the second she saw me that I was the dog for their family. And she and Cori tell Benita the whole story of how Molly found her mother while the boss and I were searching for bed bugs and Cori was working undercover, and how I got shot and everything.

As I said, dinner lasts a *long* time. At the end, just as they push back their chairs and start carrying dishes to the sink, Molly says, "I brought Scrabble. D—Dad says you like to play."

If Cori hears how Molly's voice suddenly got stringy with tension she doesn't show it.

"Scrabble? Haven't played that in years." She smiles down on her daughter. "Yeah, we could do that. Benita here used to be a ruthless player."

Benita's scratchy laugh carries over the running water of the dishes she's rinsing. "I had to be, to beat you."

"And we could make popcorn." Molly says.

Cori glances at her cupboards. "I don't know if I have—"

"I brought some bags. In case we wanted some. And some chocolate almonds."

Cori raises her eyebrows in surprise. "Okay," she says, in an amused tone, "popcorn and candy and Scrabble."

Benita sighs. "Oh, *Chica,* how I wish I could stay! Any other time, I could. But it's our big rummage sale at St. Michael's this weekend. We've been working on it all year." She glances up at the clock on the wall. "In fact, I need to get moving. Anita and I have to finish pricing the men's clothing tonight, and I have to be at the church at seven tomorrow."

"It's okay," Molly says, bending to put a glass into the dishwasher.

Benita wipes her hands, and then takes Molly's hands in hers. "But come visit again when I have more time. Promise me, *Chica*?"

Molly nods.

"And I can beat you both at Scrabble."

Molly manages a smile at this. Benita grabs a purse and some keys from the kitchen counter, and with a few more good-byes, leaves through the side door. "Don't wait up," she says.

Watching her go, Molly says, "I guess I should feed Doodle."

Good idea. I click alongside her down the shiny wood floors as she carries the plastic bucket filled with my food from where we left it in the entryway. As usual, I'd rather have what everyone just ate, but kibble it is. But then Molly grabs her plate from the counter and scrapes part of an enchilada on top of that. Have I mentioned she's good for that?

As I start eating, Miga heads straight for my dish as if she's going to share my food. Rubbing my legs is one thing. Stealing my food is another. Not Going To Happen. I curl my lip and give her a stare that leaves no question of my intent if she comes any closer. For once, she gets it. She puffs up a little, in that way cats do, and walks haughtily away as if she'd never intended to come any closer.

Still, I hurry through the meal before there are any more interruptions. Then, Molly takes me outside to the tiny back yard to do my business. I go to the furthest corner, which isn't far at all, and stinks of strange cats. As we're coming back through the door, Cori's phone emits an angry-sounding squawk.

Cori peers at the display, frowning as she flips it open. "Vega." She listens for a moment, her frown deepening. I can hear the voice on the other end but can't make out the words. Beside me, Molly has gone very still.

"Have you tried Ortega?" More listening. "What about Nelson?" She bites her lower lip and sighs. "It's not good for me. I have … complications. Yeah. Yeah, I understand." She glances at Molly, her eyes troubled. "Okay, I'll let you know." More listening. "Downtown, by the 7-11. Got it. I … I got to make some arrangements here. I'll call you back."

She snaps it shut and turns to Molly. "They need me to go in. Two people called in sick with this flu that's going around, and they have a robbery at the Macy's downtown."

Molly's voice has a faint tremor. "Okay."

Cori must hear it. "I'm sorry, Molly. This … this is why I hesitated to have you come over. I was afraid of something like this…" She shakes her head. "The job's the job. Nothing I can do about it. But what am I going to do with you?"

"I could stay here," Molly offers. "It'll only be a few hours until Benita comes home. Doodle will keep me comp—"

Cori, shaking her head, interrupts. "Absolutely not. There's no way I can leave you alone."

"But I'm ten. I often stay—"

"No." She shuts her eyes, thinking. "Where's that list from your father? Maybe his sister-in-law..." She hurries from the room.

"Oh, Doodle." Molly's voice breaks on the last part of my name. I come over and lick her hand. She swipes at her eyes, takes a deep breath, stares at her feet, and then says, "Tanya."

By the time Cori returns, holding a paper in one hand and her cell in the other, Molly is talking on the phone.

"Could you ask your mom?" she's saying. "It's sort of an emergency." While she waits, Cori raises her eyebrows. "Who's that?"

Molly says, "Tanya Franklin. My best friend. I'm seeing if I can go to her house." At Cori's expression, Molly adds, "You know her mom. From when you were working at Serene Vista?"

Cori stares a second. "*Barbara* Franklin? The manager?"

Molly head bobs up and down. "Yeah. She's Tanya's mom."

The phone squawks and Molly says, "Yeah," then brightens slightly. "Good. Thanks. We'll—I forgot to say I have Doodle—we'll be there pretty soon."

"I don't see the name on the list," Cori says, not sounding convinced. She and Molly discuss it some more, and then Cori ends up calling Mrs. Franklin herself. After that, she makes a few other calls before she and Molly begin to stow our stuff into the trunk of her car. She doesn't have a van like we do, so Molly puts me on the back seat, and the next thing I know, we're on our way to the Franklin's.

Chapter 13

Change of Plans

WE DON'T GET FAR BEFORE CORI'S PHONE EMITS that awful buzzing. Cori pushes a button on the dashboard and says, "Vega."

Hey, now the sound of the caller's voice comes from the car, like it's one of the boss's radio programs.

"Ferguson here," a man's voice says. "We got a couple of suspects we're taking to the station. A couple of teenagers after drug money. We caught them a few blocks away with a stash—pot and coke. We're getting fingerprints now to see if it matches the ones on the cash register."

"Good. I'll stop by the scene and then meet you at the station." She pushes a button and the sound stops.

"So, they already solved the crime?" Molly's voice is edged with hope

"I wish it were that easy," Cori says. "But this is just the beginning. Having a suspect and building a solid case are two different things." She shakes her head. "Sad." Her voice thickens with emotion. "I hate drugs. Especially drugs and kids."

Molly leans forward with sudden interest. “What happens to the drugs?”

“They’re tagged and go into the Evidence drawer.”

Molly thinks a minute and then asks, “When people train dogs to find drugs, where do they get the drugs? From the police after the drugs aren’t needed as evidence?”

Cori gives Molly a curious glance. “Some of the K-9 unit trainers begin with Pseudo—that’s with a P like the word for *fake* or *imitation*—substances chemically designed to smell like the actual drugs. Then they move on to having the dogs train on the real thing.”

“Where do they get those?”

“The Pseudo’s available online. The real stuff they get from agencies that control drugs used for training. They have to have department approval.” Another glance. “Why?”

“Just wondering,” Molly says, her face toward the window. “Just a few more blocks now.”

“Just wondering?’ Cori presses.

I can hear Molly’s heart speed up. “This friend of my dad’s, that he’s, um, sort of seeing—” Molly turns and studies her mother’s face “—Annie Hanson’s her name. Anyway, she’s teaching me how to train dogs to find bed bugs and she has all these vials with live and dead bugs. I just wondered when they train drug dogs where they get the drugs for training.”

Molly jabs a finger toward the windshield. “That’s it. The white house with the van.”

Mrs. Franklin and Tanya meet us in the driveway before Cori even has a chance to turn off the engine. While the two women talk, Molly gets me out of the car, and she and Tanya lug all our stuff inside.

"Are you staying the whole weekend?" Tanya asks, appearing delighted at the prospect.

"Probably." Molly says the word as if it has a bitter taste. "Probably my only visit ever and it's already over."

"Oh. Sorry." Tanya says, her face sympathetic.

"But I found out about where to get the stuff to train Doodle. So he can find the pot and clear Kenny." I lift my ears at the sound of my name, but Molly just repeats the conversation she had with her mother. The next thing I know they move to Tanya's computer.

"Pseudo. With a P," Molly says while Tanya types. I doze off. Clearly any training isn't going to happen right now.

I wake up when Tanya wails, "Sixty bucks! Plus shipping?"

Molly says, "Maybe there are other brands that are cheaper."

I'm just settling back to sleep when a sudden rapping on the door startles me.

"No bark!" Molly says.

Oops. Just Derrin. Don't know how I missed that. I wag my tail in apology.

He walks in, shoulders stooped, as if carrying a heavy weight. "Any luck?" He asks. Then, at Molly's questioning glance, he bends his head toward me. "Tanya told me 'bout training him."

I sit up. Are we finally going to get to that training—which always involves treats? Evidently not, because they just keep talking. I lie back down.

"Sixty dollars?" Derrin says after a bit. "I can get you some real stuff way cheaper than that—and don't ask me how I know. Not because I ever do that sh—" he catches himself, "that stuff."

He shakes his head and sighs "I'll get it for you," he says. "But don't tell no one. Not a soul. Got it?"

Molly and Tanya, both wide-eyed, nod.

Derrin leaves, his heavy footsteps thudding on the wood floor.

After that, it's bedtime. Molly sleeps on a pad on the floor beside Tanya's bed, and I sleep on a rug beside her. I kind of like having her scent so close to my nose all night.

But before I know it, the sun's glowing behind the blinds and the aroma of bacon fills the house.

Bacon is a truly wonderful food, and one of those rare ones that I prefer to eat cooked rather than raw. And this turns out to be my lucky day because Mrs. Franklin gives me half a piece and a nice-sized clump of eggs.

"Don't tell your daddy," she says to Molly, who nods, grinning at this.

Some time after lunch, which for me meant half of Molly's peanut butter sandwich, I'm lying in the sun in the backyard, absorbing the heat into my fur, when Molly bursts through the door.

"We get to go back!" she says, her face alive with happiness. "To my mom's. She solved the case."

Before long, I'm once again in the back seat of Cori's car, taking in the strong aroma of Chinese take-out. I nap for most of the trip so it seems like no time at all before we're pulling into her driveway.

We head straight to the kitchen where soon Cori and Molly are spooning big servings of food onto their plates. Molly shovels food into her mouth like a dog who's missed a few too many meals—come to think of it, Molly *has* given me most of her food over the last few days—so maybe she's pretty hungry. I suspect she's not going to leave any for me.

Cori says, "Nice family, the Franklins. They certainly saved my bacon."

I lift my head at this, but I can smell bacon a block away, and there's certainly none in this house.

"They're a great family," Molly agrees, wiping a bit of sauce from her mouth. "But now they have…" she puts down her fork, studies her mother a second and says, "Maybe you could help them back."

"How?" Cori asks.

Molly leans forward and eagerly launches into the whole account of the drugs being found in Kenny's locker. "He as good as admitted to me and Tanya that it was Justin Everly, who had his locker combination," Molly says at the end. "But he won't tell on him, and now the police say they're going to press charges."

"This is at your school, the science academy?"

"Yeah."

Cori pushes her hair back from her forehead, then twists a strand for a moment. Hey. Just like Molly. "I know your friend says he's innocent, but no one—well, hardly anyone—ever says they're guilty. He might not want to admit that to his family, you know? You'd be surprised how many people who look like the pillars of their community have secrets."

"But not Kenny. Basketball is his *life*. He wouldn't do anything that would hurt his playing. He won't even drink soda because he says it affects his endurance."

Cori doesn't look convinced.

"And here's something else," Molly continues. "His coach? Brandon Thatcher? He told Kenny not to tell the police that

Justin had the combination to his locker. He told Kenny that if he did, he'd lose the respect of the entire team."

Cori's eyes narrow with interest. "What an odd thing to tell him," she says. "Do you think he's protecting Justin for some reason? Is he the star player or something?"

Molly shakes her head. "He's not even a starter."

Cori thinks for a moment and twists her hair. "It's a different department, of course. But I could call and see who's in charge of the case. See what they have on Kenny."

"Could you?" Molly practically glows at this.

"But don't get your hopes up. Like I said, sometimes even the most perfect-looking people have secrets. And it's not my jurisdiction, so they might not give me much information."

Cori rises and carries her dish to the counter. Molly does the same. Nothing to scrape in my dish, I notice, and dinner for me is plain kibble, which I eat while they wash the dishes.

That's another thing about humans, always worrying about washing everything—dishes, clothes, dogs, even themselves. It's like they enjoy making work for themselves. I mean, I could lick those dishes perfectly clean if they'd just let me, and get a taste of that Chinese food.

After Molly and I come back in from my nightly trip outside, Cori asks, "Scrabble now? Or would you rather look at some photos of your family in Mexico?"

"Oh, photos," Molly says, brightening. "I don't have *any* of this … of your … side of the family."

So they settle down on the couch with a big book between them, while I curl up on a braided rug near Molly's feet.

"Here's my mother," Cori says, "On her wedding day."

"She's beautiful," Molly breathes, clearly enthralled.

The conversation goes on like this for some time. I doze off, only to wake up some time later to a strange sound. The floor seems to be vibrating. Wait. I know that sound! *Purring.* And that smell! I jerk my head up. Miga has snuggled down right against my front leg.

I give her a stare, then nudge her with my nose. Be gone, I say as clearly as if one of humans had spoken the words aloud.

But this cat seems to understand nothing about the natural boundaries that exist—at least that *should* exist—between cat and dog. She moves back against me, purring even louder.

Really. I jump up and move to the far end of the rug. Fortunately, she doesn't follow, and the next thing I know Molly is calling me.

I wake up hearing Molly say the word "game." I lift my head. I'm not as big on chasing the ball as some dogs, but I could be up for it.

But Cori shakes her head, yawning. "Long day. And I promised I'd go in tomorrow afternoon. After your dad picks you up." Her voice sags with exhaustion. She pushes her hair back from her face. "I don't think I'll be any good for Scrabble tonight. I'm not sure I can even remember how to spell my name."

Oh. Scrabble again. I prepare to take another nap, but Molly says, "Come on. Let's go out before you go to bed."

When we come back in, Cori shows us to a room upstairs with more shiny wood floors, a desk, and a couch pulled out to make a bed. The room smells like floor cleaner and, very faintly, of moth balls, a particularly nasty odor that clings to the bedspread. Although my crate is still folded up in the entryway, both she and Molly decide not to set it up.

"It won't really fit," Molly says. "And I brought his rug. He usually sleeps on that anyway."

Fine by me. I circle down on my rug next to Molly, ready to sleep through until morning. Which I might have except that sometime in the middle of the night, I'm awakened again by Miga's loud purring. Once again, she's curled up against my paws. I should teach her a lesson about proper cat behavior. I really should. But I'm groggy, too tired to move, and anyway, she's warming my leg. I drift back to sleep thinking that she's either one nervy or exceptionally clueless cat.

Chapter 14

An Unexpected Find

WHAT A WEEK! EVERY DAY WE GO TO TANYA'S, AS soon as Molly gets home from school, she gets a snack, and gets her chores done. Then she stuffs a couple of handfuls of my training treats—the wonderful liver ones—into her backpack, puts on my collar, grabs my leash, and off we go. Sometimes the boss drives us, but most days we walk, which naturally I prefer.

The treats surprise me on the first day, because according to the boss, they're expensive. He's always after Molly to save them for training and use dog biscuits the rest of the time.

But not long after we get to the Franklin's, I understand. Tanya greets us as we come up to the porch. "Mama has to work till eight and Daddy don't get home 'til six-thirty, so we're safe," she whispers, looking as guilty as a dog who's been caught getting into the trash. I have no idea why.

"Did you hide them?" Molly wears the same guilty expression and casts furtive glances over her shoulder. Their anxiety makes the hair on my back prickle. Are they expecting intruders? I sample the air but don't smell anything out of the ordinary.

"Yeah, in three easy places like you said. In back."

"And Tyson?"

"Gone to B.J.'s 'til supper. They're working on a poster for the second grade bake sale."

"Great," Molly says.

Instead of going inside the front door like we normally do, Molly leads me through a side gate into the yard. She digs into her backpack and pulls out some of the liver treats. Okay, now I'm interested, even though I don't know what's going on. Then she pulls out a harness. Hey, it's the one she borrowed from Annie. She clips the harness on me, and moves the leash from the pinch collar to the harness. Can't say I mind that.

Tanya pulls something out of her pocket that looks like a dried plant and hands it to Molly. "You want me inside?"

"You'd better," Molly says apologetically. "Just so you don't give anything away."

Molly waits while until the screen door creaks shut behind Tanya, then turns to me.

"Sit," Molly commands me.

For a *liver* treat? You bet.

But she doesn't give me the treat. Instead, she waves the dried sprig under my nose. "Smell." I know the command, of course, from my scent training work. I take a few sniffs and instantly think about my second boss, the one I've mentioned before. Pot. He'd smoke it when he didn't have his good friend, Jim Beam, around.

"Find," Molly says.

So that's what we're doing. From the corner of my eye, I see a motion in the kitchen window. Tanya's watching through the glass.

I raise my head and sample the air in the yard. The strongest scents are human—Molly, Tanya, Derrin. More faintly, Tyson and Mr. Franklin, the charcoal in the grill which still smells of hot dog, the grassy/muddy/sticky/leafy/buggy smell of the yard itself. As I search, I discover where I relieved myself the other day even though Molly scooped it up, and I catch the trail of one of the neighborhood cats.

But none of these is what I'm supposed to find. So I cast about some more until I hit on that particular plant scent. Over here … I lead Molly to the barbecue, where, inside, hiding in all that hot-doggy charcoal scent, is a small plastic baggie containing some of the pot.

"*Good* boy!" Molly, clearly delighted, gives me several treats. She drops the bag into her backpack, then gives the Find command again.

This time, I find the pot taped on the underside of a plastic lawn chair. Two more treats and another command to search. This one takes a little more time, but I finally find it over along the fence under a sunk-in soccer ball. (Just to be clear, it was that way when I found it. I didn't puncture this one.)

"Doodle, you're *great*!" Molly gives me half a handful of treats, one after the other, and then pats me on the back. What fun! Tanya rushes out, the screen door squeaking behind her.

"You're one smart dog," she tells me.

Can't say I disagree. And I don't even mind when she throws her arms around my neck and gives me a big hug. Tanya has a nice scent—faintly soapy with just the tiniest bit of some flowery perfume. And, today, overlaid with peanut butter. "You're going to catch that Justin Everly. I know it. And Kenny will get to come home."

"We still need a lot more practice," Molly says, but her face beams with happiness. "These were easy to find. And we're going to have to work him indoors so he's not thrown by being inside the school."

"I'll make them harder this time," Tanya says.

"But not too hard, yet. We don't want him to get discouraged." Molly leads me through the screen door into the kitchen. She takes me into the dining room, where she plops down on one of the chairs, and pulls her phone from a pocket on her windbreaker.

Did I mention that I have good hearing? That's why I'm not surprised when Tanya suddenly rushes in just as Molly's flipping her phone open.

"Mama's home!" she wails in a half-whisper. She holds up the three baggies as if they're suddenly hot. "What do we *do*?"

"My backpack's outside," Molly says.

The front door opens. The floor creaks under Mrs. Franklin's footsteps. Molly drops her phone on the table, grabs the baggies and shoves them into the pocket of her windbreaker, just as Mrs. Franklin comes in carrying two bags of groceries.

I jump up to greet her, dragging the leash. "Off!" Mrs. Franklin says. What? I hadn't actually touched her. But I back away a bit, sniffing at the beef in one of the sacks. "Hi, girls. What you up to today?"

Molly and Tanya exchange a guilty look. "Nothin'," Tanya says, her voice several notches higher than normal. Mrs. Franklin doesn't seem to notice. She sets the bags on a counter and starts putting things in the fridge. The meat goes first, I notice.

"You're home early." Tanya makes it sound like an accusation and this time Mrs. Franklin turns and gives her daughter a speculative look. "What you two been doing?" she asks, her eyes narrowing a bit.

"Nothin'," Tanya insists. "Well, training Doodle here to find—" she frowns as if thinking hard.

Molly scans the room, then looks down at the table. "My cell phone," she says at last. Tanya breathes a tiny sigh of relief.

Huh? The phone? I think I would have remembered that, even though dogs on the whole aren't supposed to have as good a memory as humans. Miguel likes to tell people it's because dogs live in the present. I don't understand that at all. What other way *is* there?

"Then if I lose it," Molly continues, "I'll just get Doodle to find it. Annie—that's Dad's friend who works with Miguel—is teaching me how to train dogs to find different things and I thought I'd start with my phone." The words pour from her as if she can't get them out quickly enough, in the way that she does when she's nervous.

Mrs. Franklin raises her eyebrows. "Can't you just call it? If you lose it?"

Molly seems taken aback by the idea, but quickly recovers. "Not if it's turned off. Or we're outside somewhere where I don't have a phone I could use."

"Oh, right." Mrs. Franklin puts a bag of carrots into the fridge and shuts the door. "How's he doing?"

"Who?" Molly asks. She blinks. "Oh, Doodle? Pretty good, I guess."

"Well, I'd like to see this. We could teach him to find Lamar's car keys. Of course, we'd have to adopt him so he could find them every other morning."

Adopt me? I like it here at the Franklin's but I'm not sure I'd want to live here. The yard is *very* small.

"So you got off early today?" Tanya asks, her voice calmer than before.

"Yeah. Mr. Norfolk screwed up the schedule. Again." Mrs. Franklin rolls her eyes. "Had LaToya come in two hours too soon. So I said I could leave early. Not that we can really afford to cut hours, with Kenny and everything. This lawyer costs…" She tightens her lips, then takes a deep breath. "Well. One day at a time, right?"

I'm lost here, but Molly and Tanya exchange a look and nod, eyes brimming with sympathy.

"So." Mrs. Franklin comes over and scratches under my chin, something I particularly like. "Can you show me your hot-shot tricks, Doodle?"

I sit, remembering the meat in the fridge. And the treats in Molly's pocket. The other one, not the one with the pot that Molly still has her hand jammed into

"Um, I'm not sure he's ready yet," Molly says. Beads of sweat form on her forehead. "He's just learning, and I don't want to overdo it."

Mrs. Franklin gives me a few more scritches. "I bet you'd do fine," she says, sounding disappointed. "A smart dog like you." She straightens up. "But I guess I'd better get dinner on."

Molly grabs my leash and we all practically flee to Tanya's bedroom. I'm not sure why. Tanya shuts the door and leans against it, scrunching up her eyes. "Oh, man. That was scary."

"Too close," Molly agrees. "We got to get my backpack."

"And the other baggie. I taped it to the backside of the hoop pole."

Molly's eyes widen. "That's totally obvious. Can you see it? From the kitchen?"

"I don't think so. You *said* not to make it too hard."

"Yeah, well," Molly picks up the leash, "we'd better get it before Tyson gets home."

"*Tyson,*" Tanya breathes with dismay. "If he finds that pot you might as well kill me right now, 'cause if you don't, Mama will." She sounds close to tears. "And she would never, *ever* forgive me."

She starts to open the door, then pauses, her fingers on the handle. "But you know Mama's going to be watching everything we do. She loves to see Doodle do his finding stuff."

Molly thinks for a moment. "How about you hide my phone, while I stay inside and talk to her? I'll keep her from looking out. You grab the baggie and stick it in my backpack. Then we'll go outside and Doodle can look for the phone." She pulls the baggies out of her pocket. "Here, stick these in the backpack, too. Down low, out of sight."

"He gonna be able to find your phone?"

Molly says, "I don't know. We haven't worked on that. Wait." She pulls out a liver treat and then rubs it all over her phone. "Maybe that will help." She thinks a minute. "Put it in the same place as the pot. So I know where it is in case I have to help him."

Help me? Again, not sure what she's talking about. All I know is that the liver treats smell really good.

"Doodle's drooling," Tanya says.

"Oh, Doodle!" Molly gives me the treat and then we all go into the kitchen. Mrs. Franklin's bent over a chopping board, cutting onions. She raises her head. "Going outside?"

"We thought we'd try Doodle one more time. On finding the phone."

If humans could read each other like dogs can, Mrs. Franklin might ask Molly why there's so much tension in her voice. But she sets the knife on the counter, grinning broadly. "This I gotta see." She pats me on the head. I try not to shrink away. "You show them Doodle-boy. Show off that nose of yours."

Molly holds out her phone for me to sniff, her hand trembling slightly. I have to say that the treats have improved it's frankly blah metallic scent quite nicely. Not too hard a place," she says, handing it to Tanya, who takes it and disappears through the door.

Molly turns to Mrs. Franklin, "He's just learning and we don't want him to get discouraged."

Discouraged? When there's liver treats? Don't think so. Although I've heard of dogs who give up on searches when they can't get a find quickly enough. But that's never happened to me. My nose always comes through.

Molly explains that it's better if the handler doesn't know where the object is hidden. "Cause we can give it away. With body language and stuff."

I'll say. Don't get me started.

Molly gives a quick nervous glance at the window and then launches into the story about Gunther and how he ended up trained to watch the handler instead of finding the object himself. And then she tells her about the marks on his neck.

"Poor dog," Mrs. Franklin says.

"Yeah," Molly says. "He needs a better home. With a good family."

"He surely does," Mrs. Franklin agrees. "But don't look at me. No money or room here for a dog."

The screen door groans and Tanya comes in carrying Molly's backpack. "I'll put this in my room where you won't forget it," she says, her casual voice at odds with the rigid set of her neck.

"Oh, good." Molly's gone rigid with tension herself. "Let's try this then."

Mrs. Franklin follows Molly and me to the backyard.

"Find phone." Molly commands.

Hmm. Why is Molly so nervous? I check the air. No scent of intruders.

"Find phone!" Molly's voice cracks a little on the word. She looks pointedly at the basketball pole.

I go toward it sniffing around the yard, circling, moving back and forth. Hey. I smell liver treats. At eye level, on the backside of the pole. I head for it but before I can even consider whether or not to alert, Molly says, "Doodle, you found it!"

I can't figure out if Molly is more amazed or relieved. Either way, her body relaxes and she gives me a huge smile.

"You *found* it! *Good* dog." She pockets her phone, which frankly could use a good licking off, doles out a series of treats and then scratches my back in that way I particularly love.

"Told you," Mrs. Franklin says. "Doodle always comes through."

So we all go back in to the house, everyone happy. When we're back in Tanya's room with the door closed, Tanya says, "I can't believe he found it. I was at the window ready to make a distraction if you needed to help him. But he just went straight to it. I can't believe it."

"Well, I helped him a little."

Hey. What?

"Still, he went right to it." Molly shakes her head. "I don't know if it was because of the liver treats or what."

I have no idea why she says that. I always get my bug, so to speak. Although, I have to admit that this time, I just followed Molly's gaze and searched there. But I'm sure I would have found it without her help. The nose never lies.

Chapter 15

A Surprise Encounter

"TODAY'S THE DAY," MOLLY WHISPERS TO ME WHEN SHE gets home from school. "We had a substitute teacher so Ms. Mandisa won't be in the room." I have no idea what she's talking about—maybe the pot-finding practice that we've doing most days—but what that has to do with Molly's teacher is beyond me.

She clicks a few keys on her computer, then the printer hums and rolls out a piece of paper.

"Harness, treats, camera, gloves," she murmurs. She shoves the pot-training harness and her camera into her backpack—and marks her paper. Then, I click along as she goes into the kitchen, where, after a couple of furtive glances towards the boss's bedroom, she scoops several handfuls of liver treats—the good ones—from the big plastic bucket into one of those zip shut bags. Promising. Maybe we're going to practice after all.

She grabs a pair of rubber gloves, sticks them and the treat bag under her shirt, and we go back to her bedroom. She drops the treats and gloves into her backpack along with my leash and my pinch collar, zips it shut, and slips into her coat. She marks the paper again, then folds it, jams it into her pocket and heads down the hall to the boss's bedroom.

"Can you take me to Tanya's now?"

He looks up from this computer, where he's been stuck all afternoon doing "paper" work, and blinks. "Tanya's?"

"Remember, we're going to work on a science project for school?" I don't think the boss can hear how Molly's heartbeat suddenly speeds up because his eyes are still focused on the monitor.

"Oh, yeah." With a sigh, he rises and shrugs into a coat. "Guess I can drop off these bills on the way." He grabs a stack of envelopes, grimacing at them. "I sure hope we get the Waddell account. I don't like feeling that we're only a few months away from being underwater."

Another mysterious statement, but the important thing is that before long we're in the van and pulling into Tanya's driveway. Molly gets me from my crate, snatches the backpack, and we head toward Tanya, who stands in the doorway.

The boss's window whirrs down and leans out. "Five okay?"

"Should be. I'll call if we run late." Tension grates at the edges of her voice.

But the boss, eyes fixed on the mirror, begins to creep the van backwards. "Okay. But not much later."

"Be careful with Doodle," he calls from the end of the driveway.

We go inside, and I start for Tanya's room, which is where we *always* go first at the Franklins, only to be surprised to feel the leash tighten. Molly stands with her back to me, watching something outside. From the tension pouring out of both Molly and Tanya, I suspect intruders, and push forward to see who's out there, the hair on my back rising. But at that moment, she whispers, "He's gone."

Who? Gone or not, neither of the girls relax, each as nervous as a cat walking past a pack of dogs. I sniff deeply but catch no scent of anyone or anything unusual.

Molly reaches into her backpack, takes out my pinch collar and fits it around my neck. Then, she puts on her coat. Hey, we're going to get a walk after all.

"Let's go," she says, still whispering.

With an anxious glance towards the kitchen, Tanya eases open the door, quietly shutting it behind us.

Outside, a cold breeze brims with scents of wood smoke, leaves, car exhaust, and rain. Molly zips her jacket and puts up her hood. "Wait. Better check the list." She digs out the paper and unfolds it. "You got your phone and the sample for Doodle?"

"Yeah." Tanya doesn't sound happy.

Molly studies her paper. "Okay. I got all my stuff."

"Let's get it over with," Tanya says. She takes off at a jog and Molly hurries to catch up. I could go much faster than either of them, four legs being superior to two in that regard, but the aptly named pinch collar reminds me not to pull. And even at the girls' slow pace, I enjoy being outside and stretching my legs.

After a couple of blocks, Tanya gasps, "Slow down," and so we walk for the next block. We turn down a side street and then another and then—hey! Just half a block ahead is the back playground of Molly's school. I wonder if they're having another career day.

Molly and Tanya bear straight past the playground to the parking lot, mostly empty with only a few cars scattered near the front. Tanya digs in her pockets, brings out her phone and says, "4:10."

"And they don't lock up until 4:30, right?"

"That's what Mrs. Rutger told me," Tanya answers. "I hope she's right."

I'm sniffing around, taking in all the great scents. Asphalt, of course, and the ever-present exhaust, but also, coming from a tall trash can by the door, chips, peanut butter & jelly, maybe fries—I crinkle my nose—definitely fries and ketchup.

Molly loops my leash over Tanya's arm. "I'll see if it's clear," she says, glancing around in every direction and then marching straight up to the door and flinging it open.

"Okay," she whispers, waving her arm at us. We rush inside, then hurry down the hall, my nails clicking on the shiny floors. I'd like to stop and sample the air, but the girls keep moving. And besides, the strongest scent other than the sharp smell of floor cleaner, wafts from Molly and Tanya—fear.

We turn down a hall and run the length of it, past the open doors of the classrooms, until Molly pulls up in front of one. She peers inside the dark room and whispers, "Safe." We go inside and Tanya eases the door shut. No one turns on the lights, but I can see well in the dark and the place smells famil—hey! It's Molly's classroom.

Molly drops my leash and then sets her backpack on the floor. She and Tanya slump down on two of the desks, puffing for breath. Come to think of it, I'm panting myself, but more from all the tension than from being tired. I treat myself to some exploratory sniffing up and down the rows of desks and in the back by the sink and trashcan.

Molly squeezes out of her coat. "I didn't think the substitute would stay late. So far so good." She pulls out her phone and stares at it a second. "4:14."

Tanya rolls her eyes. "It's gonna be a long fifteen minutes. And a long rest-of-our life if someone sees us."

Again, no clue what she's talking about. But neither of them seems inclined to move from their chairs, so after a bit, I lie down.

Molly reads over the paper again and punches keys on her phone. "You have my dad's number?"

Tanya nods.

"And I have your mom's. In case we get caught or something and one of us needs to call."

"We get caught, I'm dead. No need to call," Tanya says. "Just send flowers to my funeral."

But Molly, her eyes still on her phone, doesn't seem to hear. "You better have my mom's number, too. And give me your dad's."

Tanya's eyebrows raise. "Why. You're the one gonna call her. If we find something."

"I don't know. In case we get caught or something and we can't get anyone else. Or one of our phones dies. Or gets dropped or something." She recites a list of numbers and Tanya's phone beeps as she taps them in. Then they reverse it, and Molly keys in Tanya's numbers.

Molly unzips her backpack. "Better get Doodle ready." She pulls out my harness and snaps it on and undoes the pinch collar. Looks like we're going to practice, after all.

Then they wait in silence, checking their phones several times a minute. Finally, Tanya says, "4:40. Think it's safe?"

Molly nods, tight-lipped. She slides the door open and sticks her head out. "Looks clear." She turns to Tanya. "Do you have it?"

Tanya reaches into a pocket and hands Molly a small plastic bag.

"Sit," Molly commands, picking up the leash.

As I sit, she opens the bag. Of course, I recognize the stuff before she waves it under my nose. Pot. Definitely going to practice.

I take a few more sniffs, lingering a bit on the scent of the liver treats in her pocket.

"Find!" She leads me through the door.

I raise my nose and test the air. Such a rich sample of odors to pick from. All those kids, each leaving behind traces of sweat and unique body scent, plus there's floor polish, dust, books, stale pizza, stale coffee, metal lockers . . . I could go on, but Molly gives the leash a tiny tug.

Right. Focus, as Miguel used to tell us. I cast about in long zigzags, searching for that one distinct scent. Nothing in this hall, nor in the classrooms that Molly has me check out.

"We'll do one side first and then come back," Molly says, as we work our way down the hall.

"Gonna take a while," Tanya answers.

I have to agree. Haven't sensed a trace of pot so far.

But, then, in the last classroom before the hall makes an intersection, as I'm weaving through the desks, I catch a whiff. Definitely something here.

"This is Mr. Thatcher's room!" Molly breathes.

I sniff my way to the big desk at the far corner of the room, then around to the drawers on the backside. There. That one.

I sit and touch my nose to the drawer. Molly gives me a treat.

"I can't believe it," Tanya says. "Coach Thatcher?"

Molly reaches for something—another treat? I'm disappointed to see her pull out a pair of rubber gloves and work her fingers into them. "Got to preserve evidence," she says. No clue as to what she means.

Molly tries the drawer. "Not locked." Then, dismay lining her voice, "It's crammed full of file folders. This could take a while."

Tanya says, "I'll watch while you look." She goes back to the doorway and stands, looking into the hall.

Molly rustles through the papers in the drawer, becoming more agitated the longer she looks. Finally, she opens it as far as it will go and tugs the leash. "Find," she commands.

The scent has pooled throughout the drawer, but have I mentioned that the nose never fails? After a few rounds of intense sniffing, I touch my nose to a section of folders. Molly lifts a few of them out, flings open the covers, pawing through the papers. "Here!" She holds up an envelope, extracts a plastic bag from it, and waves it with a triumphant grin.

"*Good* dog!" she says, reaching into her pocket. And then, in a scared voice, "Who'd have thought Mr. Thatcher?"

I lift my nose for a treat, but instead she whips out her phone. "Calling my mom," she says to Tanya. She fumbles a moment. "These gloves," she mutters. Then, with a low wail, "No signal!"

Tanya tries her phone. "Me neither."

"Okay. I'll get a few shots and we'll call her when we get out." Molly's hand goes back into her pocket. Has she finally remembered my treat? I guess not because now she brings up her camera and starts clicking it at the bag, the envelope, the file drawer, the desk.

But I hear another sound, not quite clicking. I tilt my head towards the door, ears up. Something outside the classroom. I sniff hard, but don't smell anything new. But the sound…

"Someone's coming!" Tanya whispers, panic edging her voice. "What if it's Mr. Thatcher?"

Molly hesitates only a second. "Almost done. Just a few more. Run. Get outside and call my mom. If he follows you, shout, and I'll go out the other way and call her."

"And leave you alone?

"I have Doodle. Hurry."

Without another word, Tanya disappears from the doorway and I hear two sets of footsteps, her fast lighter ones and the heavier ones.

Molly casts anxious glances at the door as she clicks her camera.

Now the heavy footsteps speed up, running straight for us. Molly definitely needs to know about this. I bark an alert.

"Doodle, *no. Hush.*" Molly wails. No clue why. I'm just keeping her informed. And this is *really important* because now the footsteps are really close.

Just then, the door swings open and a man I've never seen walks in, though I've caught his scent here and there as I've searched. A cop? He wears a uniform. Stocky, but with just a slight bulge at the waist line, he's bald except for a neatly trimmed fringe of white hair around the base of his head. He smells strongly of floor cleaner. He peers at us through oval, wire-rimmed glasses.

"What's going on?" He makes it sound more like an accusation than a question, his voice full of quiet authority.

Molly gives a fleeting glance at the door. She seems at once relieved and anxious. “Oh. Mr. Olsen,” she said. “Don’t you—don’t the janitors leave at 4:30?”

Oh. The janitor.

“I forgot my thermos and came—but—” He shakes his head. “What are *you* doing here?”

Molly launches into an explanation about Kenny and pot, and finding out who did it. “And he led us straight to the desk, and then we found pot in one of the folders.”

As soon as she says pot, Mr. Olsen comes forward and peers down at the open file folder. And, in a flash, he has his phone out. “Ms. Hernandez? Eric Olsen. I think you might want to come and look at what, um, has been found in one of the teacher’s rooms.” He starts to tell her about Molly, but just at that point, I see a motion. Why it’s Tanya. She peeks around the door frame, then rushes in.

“Oh. It’s just Mr. Olsen. I thought it was Mr. Thatcher and he might kidnap you or something so I ran outside and called your mom. And your dad. And then came back to see if you escaped. But I guess—” Tanya’s eyes go from Molly to the janitor”—I guess you’re okay.”

“And Mr. Olsen called the principal,” Molly says in a glum voice.

“We’re in trouble now,” Tanya says.

“Probably,” Molly agrees. “But maybe not as much as Mr. Thatcher.”

Chapter 16

Everybody's Mad

THE PRINCIPAL, A SHORT-ROUND HISPANIC WOMAN with graying hair and a no-nonsense expression, arrives first, takes one look at the pot and calls the police. While we're waiting she lectures Molly and Tanya about sneaking into the school after hours.

"It wasn't locked," Tanya retorts at one point.

The principal glares at her in the way that a Rottweiler might look at an annoying, yappy dog.

And then Molly's mother comes running into the room, flushed and breathless. "Are you okay?" She stops, takes in the scene, then listens stone-faced while Mr. Olsen explains the situation.

"What the hell did you two think you were doing?" she asks Molly and Tanya.

Molly's face pales—whether from the anger in her mother's voice or the fact that she used "language." She leans into me, her face against my shoulder. "Clearing Kenny," she says into my fur. "We *knew* he wasn't the one selling drugs. Now we know it's Mr. Thatcher. No wonder he told Kenny not to be a snitch."

Molly explains how she trained me to find pot and how I led her here. When she finishes, Cori just keeps shaking her head.

"You might have just made a mess of it all. Who knows whether any of this evidence will hold up. And what if you had run into Mr. Thatcher? You could have been hurt—" here her voice trembles slightly "—or even worse. Not smart at all. You *really* need to leave this kind of stuff to the cops."

"She wore gloves," Tanya offers in a nervous voice. "And photographed everything in Mr. Thatcher's desk."

"Well, we'll see if any of this holds up. His attorney could claim that you planted the evidence to try to clear Kenny."

Molly's grip on my fur tightens. "We thought the police would want to know who did it. Who *really* did it."

Cori closes her eyes, takes a long breath and lets it out slowly. "We do want to know that," she says in a softer voice. "But people can't take the law into their own hands. It's too dangerous for everyone. That's why we have police and law enforcement: professionals who know the right way to do the job."

Something hits my paw. Why, it's a tear. Now that I think about it, I can feel a wet spot where Molly's face digs into my fur.

With a clatter of boots on tile, the cops come next, four of them who swarm around the desk.

Cori pulls the one in charge aside and talks to him in a low voice. I try to hear what she's saying, but then I hear the boss's voice.

"Moll, are you all right?" he asks, red-faced and puffing.

Molly swipes a hand across her eyes before turning toward him. "Yeah. We're fine."

"Tanya's call—" he seems unable to speak for a moment. "Scared me half to death." He pulls her into an awkward hug, then releases her. He studies the room a second, looking puzzled. "Cori's here? And where's Thatcher?"

Tanya says in a small voice, "I'm so sorry, Mr. Hunter. I thought Mr. Thatcher was after us, but it was just the janitor."

The boss blinks, as if he can't take it in.

Cori leaves the cop and comes over to Molly and Tanya. "Oh, good," she says to the boss. "Glad you're here. I need to get back, but didn't want to leave them until you came. I told Sgt. Reardon over there to go easy on the girls when he takes their statements." She grimaces when her phone buzzes and punches a button that silences it.

"Not that they deserve it." She gives Molly and Tanya a stern look. "You're both very lucky. Anyway, I've—" Her phone buzzes again. She shakes her head. "I really have to go." She hurries through the door, her cell to her ear.

The boss watches her leave, then turns to Molly. "But what were you doing here?"

"Clearing Kenny." Molly glances at Tanya, who nods in agreement. "We trained Doodle to find pot, and then when we did a search, he found it in Mr. Thatcher's desk."

The boss's mouth opens but no words come out. I can smell his anger. Finally, he says, "You *what*?"

"Trained Doodle. Tanya and I." Molly's words tumble out the way they do when she's nervous. "But I talked to Annie and I was really careful. I asked her about cross-training and did everything she said—used a different harness, and different commands—so he wouldn't get confused about bed bugs."

The boss frowns as if he can't quite take it in. "*Annie* knows?"

"Well, not exactly. I mean she knows I wanted to learn to train dogs, but not about this…"

"We trained him ourselves," Tanya adds with pride. "And when we told him to find the pot, he went straight to it. Straight to Mr. Thatcher's desk."

Really? Because I remember searching a bunch of rooms first. Maybe Tanya forgot.

Tanya leans over and pats my side. "You're such a *good* dog."

The boss glowers at Molly and Tanya in a way that could make a dog slink away, tail between his legs. "And you didn't think that maybe training him on something new might keep him from passing his certs?"

"Annie says dogs are trained for more than one scent all the time."

"Pot," he mutters. He puts his head in his hands, rubbing his forehead. "Where'd you get *that*?"

Molly and Tanya pass a guilty look. "From someone we know," Molly says at last. "Who knew what we were trying to do. But we gave the training sample to the cops. Soon as they got here."

Tanya nods emphatically. "We'd never, *ever* use it."

They talk some more, but frankly, I'm tired. I lay my head on my paws. The next thing I know, a strident voice bellows "Where'd you get *pot*?"

Mrs. Franklin glares down at Molly and Tanya, every bit as angry as the boss was earlier. When did she get here? I must have dozed off. She goes on for some time about how much trouble the girls are in.

Turns out everyone is mad at Molly and Tanya. Cori, the boss, Mrs. Franklin, the other cops, the principal, and the janitor. And they all take turns telling the girls why.

So when we finally get to leave, Molly and the boss walk to the van in a tense silence that doesn't let up for the entire trip home.

In the morning, Molly stays home even though it's a school day. When she first got up, she told the boss she didn't feel well enough to go, and he just nodded and went back to his office without another word.

We pretty much spend the entire day in her room, which is fine by me, except, of course, a walk would be nice. But even though I remind her several times, she doesn't seem interested. And with the boss in his current mood, it's best to keep to ourselves. She mopes about, going from her computer to her bed, her face masked in a sadness that occasionally gives way to tears.

Then, in the afternoon, her phone rings. "Tanya's home!" Molly says with the first sign of enthusiasm she's had all day. She puffs up her pillows on the bed and leans back as she puts her phone to her ear.

Tanya's voice comes through sounding faintly metallic but otherwise perfectly clear. "Where *were* you? I looked for you all day."

"Didn't feel good. How was school?"

"Police here all morning. They had dogs go through all the lockers again, and then—guess what?" Tanya doesn't wait for a guess. "They took Justin Everly to the station. And we had an assembly and the principal went through all the zero tolerance stuff and said there'd be changes. And Mr. Thatcher's classes had a substitute."

"That's good," Molly says. "If they don't dismiss all the charges."

"Mama says our lawyer doesn't think they will. She said that after the cops left, they did some kind of sting and caught Mr. Thatcher with some of the drugs in his pocket or something. Enough to at least get him fired. But guess what else? Even better?"

This time Molly gets in a word. "What?"

"Kenny's home!"

"What? How?" Molly sits straight up, suddenly alert.

"When he heard that Coach Thatcher had the drugs, then he knew all that stuff Coach was telling him about not snitching was just so Coach wouldn't get caught, and Kenny got good and mad, and told them about Justin Everly, and then I guess Justin Everly told on Coach Thatcher and said he was the one in charge of it all. And Justin said Kenny had nothing to do with it. So they released him."

For the first time today, Molly's face breaks into a smile. "That's wonderful!"

"Yeah, worth being on restriction for—which I might be for the rest of my life the way Mama is going on."

"Me too. With my dad, I mean. He said—"

But Tanya interrupts. "Wait. Kenny's here. He wants to talk to you."

After a brief pause, I hear Kenny's voice. "Hey, Molly."

"You're home!" Molly says.

"Yeah. Thanks to you. What you and Tanya did—" Kenny's voice thickens and he takes a deep breath.

"Derrin helped, too, but don't tell your mom."

"I know," Kenny says. "Tanya told me. I just want to say thanks. I mean it. You're two gutsy girls."

Now Molly's grin practically splits her face.

"And pet The Dude for me."

I can't help but wag my tail.

"You and Tanya, you're in my book. I owe you. You know?"

"Okay," Molly says.

And then Tanya's voice is back. She and Molly talk for some time but I doze off.

When she finally gets off the phone, Molly says, "I'm hungry." No surprise there, since she gave me most of her cereal this morning when the boss wasn't looking. I follow her toward the kitchen.

From his bedroom, the boss says, "So you don't think it'll be a problem?

Molly stops dead just outside the kitchen door, listening. I wait for her to answer but then realize that the boss is on the phone.

I tilt my head and perk my ears, but he's too far away for me to hear who he's talking to.

"Well, I hope you're right. The next test isn't for six months."

Another pause and then he says, "You're right. She's a great kid. And the most important thing is that she's okay. Scared me to death, you know? I'll just feel better when we have our certification. Sometimes I think this whole venture's a house of cards."

Lost me there. Cards? But now his footsteps creak on the floor boards.

Molly bolts into the kitchen, flings open the cupboard and takes out the peanut butter. She's spreading it on a piece of bread when the boss walks in, phone still to his ear. "Thanks, Annie. I appreciate it. It's . . . it's good to have someone to talk to."

He snaps the phone shut, then clears his throat.

"Just talked to Annie. She thinks Doodle will be okay for the test. As far as scent confusion goes."

Molly nods, starts to speak, then falls silent.

"What?" the boss asks.

"Kenny's home. Justin Everly confessed."

The boss manages a brief smile. "That's good, at least." And then, as Molly sucks in her breath, he adds, "That's more than good. What a relief. The Franklins must be ecstatic."

He reaches into the cupboard by the back door where he keeps the bed bug vials. I perk up my ears. Looks like we're going to practice.

"To be safe, I'm going to work him three times a day until the test. That'll give us twenty-one practices, and Annie said I could do some over at her place for variety. No use going in unprepared."

Molly nods again, and takes a bite of her sandwich while the boss starts setting things up for a practice.

Which turns out to be easy. Piece of cake, to use the boss's words, although in my case the pieces turn out to be the liver treats I earn by finding the vials.

"I guess you still know how to do it," he says, when we're done. The muscles in his neck relax for the first time since he came running into the school.

Not sure why he ever doubts me. Finding bed bugs is what I do best.

Chapter 17

Dead-Bugged

"WHAT THE—?" THE BOSS HOLDS UP THE BAG OF liver treats. "I know I used a lot practicing this week, but I thought we had one more 3-pack. Did you use a whole *bag* with your pot training?"

The boss glares through the kitchen door. Today is the day of the cert trial and, frankly, the boss isn't handling the pressure very well. He's been nervous as a cat in a room full of rocking chairs, as my first boss used to say.

Molly comes in from her bedroom carrying her backpack and my rug, the one I sleep on in her room. Both she and the boss have been packing. Turns out that Sid's place, where I'm taking the test, is just down the road from Miguel's and he invited us to spend the night after the test so we don't have to drive home in traffic.

Molly nods. "We had to practice a lot."

He frowns. "You know these things cost an arm and a leg."

First time I heard the boss use this expression, I was a little repulsed, but it turns out it's just another way of saying a lot of money.

The boss drops the bag into the plastic bucket with my food and snaps down the lid. "This is barely going to be enough for this afternoon." He frowns. "I better call Annie and see if she has some I can buy from her."

Judging by how often he does it, which is several times a day, the boss hardly needs an excuse to call Annie. Now, he talks to her briefly and then clips his phone shut. "She has plenty," he says, sounding considerably more cheerful. He grabs the bucket by the handle and heads for the door. "Got everything? A coat? It'll be chilly tonight and tomorrow it will be even colder. Chloe's the second one up."

That's the other reason that we're spending the night at Miguel's, so we can go watch Annie and Chloe have their trial in the morning without worrying about traffic. As I think I've said before, nothing the boss hates worse.

"Annie's bringing salad and banana pudding tonight," he says happily, "and Miguel's making his famous sourdough bread. We'll add the chicken. It'll be a feast."

Soon we're all in the van. I settle down and have a nice nap until the boss's voice, loud and annoyed, wakes me up. "How can 66 be backed up *this* time of day?"

We're in a long line of cars going very slowly. The boss's fingers tap the wheel in nervous, sporadic patterns. "Two hours early," he mutters, "and we're barely going to be there in time." He continues to tap and mutter, even using some "language", which he rarely does, until finally the van picks up speed again.

I stretch as much as the space in my crate will allow and circle down to sleep some more. The next thing I know the van is slowing to a stop.

"I guess this is it. Smithfield's Sniffer Dogs: Training and Boarding." He turns the van onto a vast black driveway that gleams in the late afternoon sun. "Wow."

Everything here seems to shine—the dark green metal roof on the long barn, the silver siding, the chainlink fences surrounding the kennels that sit back behind the barn. Rows of young trees line the driveway, and flower beds I bet dogs are *never* allowed near, flank both sides of the barn's double doors.

The van creeps down a graveled parking area, between two rows of trucks and vans. "Sid got himself a nice gig. The owner must have serious money." He pulls alongside a big SUV, turns off the engine, and glances at his watch, shaking his head. "We're up in 45 minutes. So much for that 'half-hour' drive and having a couple of hours here to relax."

He clips on my leash, unloads me from the crate, and we all start for the big double doors. What a place. Brimming over with interesting scents. Lots of people I don't know, all sorts of smells from dogs I've never met, not to mention all the car exhaust, the leaves and leaf-mold, grass, mulch and the highly aromatic portable toilets that sit in little columns off to the side of the barn.

"Doodle, don't *pull!* Heel!" The boss glances around the parking lot, something he's been doing every few steps since we left the van. "Do you see Annie?" he asks Molly. "She said she'd be here at least an hour—"

"Josh!" The voice is Annie's but the smell—that unmistakable sickly sweet cologne—comes from Sid.

Annie waves from just inside the doors. As we hurry to meet her, Sid suddenly surges from behind, his odor engulfing us. Pity the poor dogs who have to do any scent detection with him nearby. Today, along with his tight jeans, open-necked shirt and gold chain, he's wearing a single earring that glints in the sun. I wonder if he lost the other. I used to find earrings, back in my service dog days.

"Hey, Josh." His eyes are cold even though his lips form a broad smile."What do you think?" His arm extends in a grand flourish. "State of the art facilities. We have a totally enclosed, floor to ceiling test area that's divided into four rooms. And a separate room with a closed-circuit TV so anyone who wants can watch the proceedings without disturbing the dog or handler during the trial. The walls are on metal tracking so they can be moved or removed if we want."

"Very nice," the boss says, looking less than convinced.

"And indoor-outdoor kennels for up to 40 dogs in the adjacent building." Sid leans forward and lowers his voice. "Not to criticize Miguel or anything, but the difference between his place and here—night and day. You can see why I recommend it."

"Not to mention you run the place," the boss says in a tight voice.

Sid waves off the remark. "Yeah, but even if I didn't—just no comparison." He bends down to Molly. "Hi there, young lady. How's my favorite little photographer doing today?"

Molly flinches ever so slightly, and the hair raises on my back.

"Did you bring your camera?"

Molly's hand steals to her pocket. She starts to pick it up, then, catching herself, lifts her hand without it.

"Ah. I see you did. I'll have to ask you to take it back to your car. We have a strict policy of no photographs here."

Molly flushes. The boss says, "If you tell her not to take photos, she—"

"I'm sorry." Sid looks more pleased than sorry. "We have to ask you to take it back to the car. Or, you can check it at the office, if you prefer. Just inside, on the left. Ramón can show you." He gestures towards the entrance where a uniformed man, big enough to be a linebacker (football—now's there's a waste of time) watches us with an expressionless face.

"I'll take it to the car." Molly's voice is strung tight with tension. "Keys?" She takes the keys and leaves without another word.

The boss's anger flows down the leash so intensely that I have to scratch my shoulder. He glowers at Sid, who's too busy scanning the premises to notice. "Oops. Got to talk to someone," he says abruptly. "Good luck." And he bustles off in the direction of the portable toilets.

By the time Molly returns, Annie has come up to us. I can smell that she remembered to bring the treats. Good thing, because I haven't had breakfast. "What'd Sid want?" she asks.

"He's a piece of work." The boss stares at Sid's retreating form, his anger still vibrating down the leash. He tells Annie about Molly's camera. "It's not whether or not cameras are allowed, it's just the way he's so … so …"

Annie nods, her eyes sympathetic. "Slimy? Did I tell you about Gunther?"

"How's he doing?" Molly asks, suddenly interested. "Is he taking the test?"

"I don't know." Annie shrugs. "He was doing much better. Not watching me to indicate where the vials were. But still not distinguishing between live and dead bugs. I asked Sid if he'd ever had a vet check him, because I wonder whether Gunther can discriminate between subtle scents the way he should."

Annie pushes her hair back from her face and grimaces.

"So what happened?" asks Molly.

"The way Sid acted, you'd have thought I was trying to steal all his clients or something. He went on about how I was interfering with his training and only making things worse, and the next thing I know he and Jerry drive up and haul Gunther off."

She sighs. "So, the short answer is, I don't know. Anyway, there's the office." She inclines her head toward a room with big glass windows off to the side of the entrance. "You need to let them know you're here. They're setting up the finds right now. Oh and—" she pats the canvas bag slung over her shoulder "—I brought the extra treats."

The boss hands the leash to Molly, and goes over to the office.

"Up in half an hour," the boss says when he returns.

"You go over there." Annie points to a wall on one side of the big room. "Where the security guard is. The door is around on the back side. We'll be watching from the viewing area."

Molly and Annie go to find seats, while the boss takes me outside. I'd like to go over by the portable toilets—so rich in scent—but the boss avoids those.

Before long, we've returned and made our way to the back of the testing area. The guard Annie pointed out earlier steps forward. A young man, skinny, with a long, knobby neck and a face pocked with acne. He wears a dark nylon windbreaker with some words and a photo of a Labrador retriever on the back.

The boss goes up to him. "Josh Hunter and Doodle," he says.

The guard checks his clipboard and motions us toward two men who also hold clipboards. Sid, fortunately, is nowhere to be seen—or, in this case, smelled—but there's something interesting about the scent of the skinny guard. I ease closer.

"Good afternoon," says one of the clipboard men. Bald, with a bushy gray moustache and thick, muscled arms, he gives the boss and me a friendly smile. I watch, fascinated, at the way his moustache moves up and down when he speaks.

"Captain Pete Carlisle," he says, "out of Fairfax. I'll be the senior evaluator and Rick Ortega here—" he points to a lean young man with short, spiked, black hair and skin the color of a chocolate Lab "—will be the second."

The boss drums his fingers against his jeans, and beads of sweat moisten his forehead.

"You'll have twenty minutes," Moustache Man says. "Ready?"

The boss coughs, clears his throat. "Yes."

Uh-oh. The tension pours off him in acrid scents. Again—no reason for him to worry. This is what I do best. And I'm glad to be doing it, because I'm very hungry and those treats in the boss's pouch smell pretty irresistible.

Moustache Man clicks the timer. "Begin."

"Find." For all his nerves, the boss gives the command in a low, calm voice.

I lift my nose and cast about, sifting out irrelevant scents, searching for that one particular odor that means live bed bugs.

Whoa. Just a few preliminary sniffs tell me of several spots in this room alone, which has a couch, several stuffed chairs, and a dining table. I thought this trial was supposed to be difficult. I hone in on the closest one, along the back bottom edge of one of the stuffed chairs. I give the alert.

"Good dog," the boss says with an anxious glance at the evaluators. He pays me with a treat.

I alert on a light fixture in the same room and on the top rim of a sofa, before moving on to the next, a bedroom, which yields a find under the pillow of the bed. By the bed, on a table, sits a leather cell phone case. I move closer, checking it out. Interesting. Dead bugs form a large part of the scent, and at first I think this is a distractor. But it also carries the odor of live bugs—although something about it is just a little off. I sniff some more. Definitely live bugs. I give the alert.

"Good boy." It's hard to believe the boss's words when he's so plainly anxious.

The next room has a crib, lots of stuffed toys, and big beanbag, which would be a great place for bed bugs to hide. But the beanbag is clean, other than a faint scent of vomit on one little spot, and root beer on another.

I move to the stuffed toys. Most have no scent, but a little one on the end smells like the phone case. It has a strong odor of dead bugs which means it's probably a distractor. But it also has a live bug smell. And, just like the phone case, this one smells slightly off. But not off in a "dead bug" or, say termite (often used as distractors) way. I give the alert.

Again, the boss praises me and rewards me with a treat, but with a drawn face. Not sure why. I mean, I'm finding the bugs, right?

The last room, done to imitate a kitchen, has no bed bugs. One of the baseboards smells like dead termites but I know enough not to be fooled.

When we're done—by "we," I mean me—the boss leads me over to the evaluators.

"Sorry," Pete says, his voice deep and gravelly. "He found all the vials, but he had two false alerts as well."

The boss stares, swallows, blinks, then looks to the other evaluator who sticks his pen into the top of the clipboard. "That's what I have, too. Two on dead bugs. The stuffed bear and the phone case."

I don't think so. I smelled live bugs. Once again, the humans get it wrong.

"Okay."

Whoa. My tail sinks at the flat, depressed sound to his voice.

The boss lifts a hand to his beard, but then drops it again. Slump-shouldered, he heads towards the stand, the leash hanging slack between us.

Molly jumps up and rushes over, Annie just behind her.

"Did he—"

"No." The word comes out almost like a bark in its ferocity. "He alerted on distractors."

Annie frowns. "I don't believe it. He's been perfect every time."

"Well, he wasn't perfect today."

Molly, pale and looking near tears, says nothing. She rests a hand on my back. "Poor Doodle," she whispers.

But the boss hears her. "Poor *us*. I don't know what we're going to do now."

Chapter 18

Miguel's

ALTHOUGH THE DRIVE TO MIGUEL'S IS A SHORT one—at least according to the boss—it feels long because of the oppressive silence in the van. And we don't go directly there. First, we pull into a fast-food place. Soon, we have two buckets of chicken that pretty much smell up the whole van.

I have a small lake of drool in my crate by the time we pull into the driveway, and my stomach is rumbling. True, I got treats at the cert trial, but not that many, and I skipped breakfast.

Miguel limps out to meet us, his weather-lined face cracked into a broad grin. I breathe in his scent. Same smell of pipe tobacco—infinitely better than cigarettes—wood smoke, garlic, yeast, and dogs. And, to a lesser extent, horses.

He slides the van door open, snaps my leash on, and opens the crate. "Doodle, *mi hombre, que tal?*" He rubs the back of my neck.

I thump my tail. Always love to see Miguel. If anyone has that mysterious "it" the boss goes on about, Miguel's the one.

Not only that, Miguel seems to be the only human not upset right now. The boss still radiates unhappiness, and sadness wraps around Molly like a blanket.

"I guess I don't need to ask how it went," Miguel says, studying their faces. "What happened?"

The boss shakes his head. "Scent confusion's the only explanation I can think of." He avoids looking at Molly, but she turns her head away all the same.

Annie drives up with Chloe, and soon everyone is headed for the house.

Molly takes me for a stroll over to a growth of weeds by the fence so I can relieve myself. Then, I follow her up a set of brick steps, onto a wood porch that runs the width of the house, and through the door into the mouth-watering scents of fresh bread and, of course, chicken.

In all the time I was at Miguel's for training, I never once came inside his home. None of us dogs did. Our place was in the kennel. Now I see that Miguel has a small but cheerful living room with a couch and two chairs that are covered with brightly patterned blankets facing a table with a small TV. Across from the entryway is an even smaller eating area which opens to a kitchen. In a little alcove behind the dining room, a computer sits on a desk.

Molly goes over to it. "Okay if I check my email?"

The boss starts to protest, but Miguel waves her on. "Go ahead," he says.

Everything looks clean and freshly painted, which is no surprise since, when I stayed with him, Miguel was always quick to haul out the paintbrush. No smell of paint, however, which is good because paint fumes kind of make me sick.

"That's a lot of chicken," Miguel says, as the boss plops two buckets on the kitchen counter and a pack of diet ginger ale on the counter. "Are there people coming I don't know about?" His tone is friendly, teasing, but the boss just shrugs morosely.

Miguel takes out a brown bottle of beer. "It's just one test. And if it were me, I'd consider the source." He opens the bottle and tilts it up for a sip.

The boss eyes Miguel's beer, like a dog watching a tasty morsel of food. He carries the pack of ginger ale to the fridge, sticks it inside and stands in the open doorway, fingering one of the brown bottles. Then, abruptly, he twists off one of the ginger ales, shuts the door, and grabs some ice from the freezer, which he clinks into a glass.

Never understood the human fascination with ice. Cold drinks aren't my thing, unless it's water, of course, and then not as cold as ice makes it. And hot drinks—don't get me started. Room temperature's the way to go as far as I'm concerned, especially when the cold drinks are things like beer and diet ginger ale.

Annie, whose eyes were fixed on the boss the whole time his were fixed on the beer, jumps as her phone begins to buzz like a giant, angry insect.

"Annie Harmon," she says in a pleasant voice.

Jerry's voice squawks from the speaker, loud enough that even the humans can hear. The boss and Miguel exchange a look. Molly leaves the computer and takes a seat at the table, clearly listening as well.

"I thought I'd tell you that Gunther got his NABBS certification this morning. He had no problem distinguishing the dead bugs from the live ones."

Annie's eyebrows raise and her mouth drops in astonishment. "Um, that's great, Jerry. Congratulations."

"So you were wrong about his nose. I'm just lucky that we took him back to Sid's before you did real damage." The anger in his voice makes me nervous, even though I know that these voices that come over the phone aren't anywhere near enough to see, much less smell. I sit up and scratch my shoulder. Much better.

"I—" Annie begins, but then seems to choke on the words. She clears her throat.

"And you can bet that I'm telling everyone I know to avoid Miguel's. Sid told me that neither of you really know what you're doing, and I can see he's right."

Annie shakes her head, still not speaking. She blinks and swipes at her eyes.

I can't help but whine. Molly glances at me. "Hush," she says softly. "Relax." But nothing in the way she sits, stiff with tension, makes me want to relax. I scratch again.

"Anyway, I just wanted to tell you. It was wrong of you to interfere with Gunther. He's a perfectly good bed bug dog." With a click the phone goes silent.

Annie snaps her phone shut, but she stands unmoving, her eyes not focused.

"The jerk," the boss says.

Miguel takes another sip of beer, a hard expression on his face.

The boss says, "That's rich. Sid gets Jerry to blame you even though you gave Gunther hours of free training."

"Yeah." Annie sounds glum. "But I put in those hours for Gunther's sake, not Jerry's. I hoped if I could get him on track, Jerry would relax and treat him better."

Miguel gives her a pitying look. "The hardest part of the job," he says softly, "is not being able to rescue dogs from bad owners. We can train the dogs, but the humans?" He shakes his head.

I think about my second boss, and have to agree.

"I can't believe he passed his trial. I would've sworn the poor dog was out of his depth." She exhales a long, shuddering breath. "Well, I guess I screwed things up royal. Now I see why you're so cautious about new clients. If you want to fire me for losing you business—"

"Don't be stupid," Miguel says, his voice as hard as the glint in his eye. "The day I take training advice from someone like Sid…" He rises, shaking his head. "Trust me."

I always trust Miguel, although in this case I'm not exactly sure what about.

He grabs a stack of paper plates and plops them on the counter next to a bowl of potato salad, and beside it, wrapped in foil, a loaf of warm bread whose tantalizing fumes already waft throughout the house. "Help yourself."

Oh, that I could.

Before long, everyone has a plate of food—every *human*, that is, and they crowd around the little table in the dining room. Chloe and I watch, drooling, from the kitchen floor, both of us alert to any morsel that might drop.

Dinner is pretty much a quiet affair. For once the humans don't talk their heads off. But for all that silence, no one seems to eat much. Chloe and I could remedy that in a hurry.

"I don't get it," Annie says after awhile. "Gunther passes and Doodle fails. I would have bet hard cash on the just the opposite."

Molly, who has been working on the same piece of chicken since she sat down, swallows and looks up with interest.

Miguel traces a line of moisture around his bottle. "Like I said before, consider the source."

"What do you mean by that?" the boss asks. He's eaten even less than Molly.

"I'd trust Sid about as far as I could throw him, and he's bigger than me. So if he's running a trial and the results are the opposite of what everyone expects, I say look to the source."

The boss shakes his head. "Don't see how anyone could rig it. Unless the judges are crooked."

"Who sets it up?" Miguel asks.

"The chief evaluator. A cop from Fairfax. Pete somebody. He's done dozens of certs."

Miguel shrugs, and no one speaks for some time.

Hey. Things are looking up. Molly tears off a piece of her chicken and folds her napkin over it. Then another. And then, she adds a piece of bread. She slips the napkin in the pocket of her jacket.

And finally, the sound we dogs have been waiting for—the scrape of chair-legs against the tile. Everyone gets up.

"Can I feed Doodle?" Molly asks.

"Sure. I haven't brought in his food." The boss tosses the keys to Molly. She clips on my leash.

As soon as we're outside, Molly feeds me the contents of her napkin. Delicious! Then she gets my kibble and dish from the van and feeds me right there. Nowhere near as tasty as the chicken, but I eat it with relish. As Miguel used to say when he'd give us treats, "hunger makes the best sauce" which I think means food tastes better if you've had to miss breakfast.

After I eat, Molly takes me over to one of the big buckets of water that sit under a faucet just inside the barn's entrance. While I lap, she flips open her phone, but then snaps it shut, going suddenly still.

I stop drinking and listen. Voices. A bark rises in my throat, but just in time I realize it's Annie and the boss. Their footsteps crunch on the gravel, the boss's voice urgent.

"I know Miguel thinks something's fishy going on with Sid—"

Fish? I test the air. I don't think so.

"—and he trained him, you know? So while I don't know a more honest man, maybe Miguel doesn't want to believe Doodle could fail."

Smart man, Miguel.

"And, anyway, he misses the point. Even if this cert isn't completely legit—and I still don't see how it can be faked—it doesn't *matter* as far as my business is concerned. Because Sid has convinced half the available clients in the area that certification means competence. We've been hanging on by a thread—all those loans to get started, and barely enough income to take care of them and Molly's school, which isn't cheap even with her scholarship. And now, if we lose even a small chunk of our business because we don't have this cert, I'm not sure how long we can hold out." He sighs and the footsteps stop. Molly stands so still I can't even hear her breathe.

"I think Doodle's problem was scent confusion. Maybe when he trained for pot, he forgot about distinguishing between live and dead bugs."

He's silent for a moment. "I don't know what to do. I mean, Molly did a great thing clearing Kenny. How can I get after her for that? She's such a good kid, got such a great heart. I just wish she could have cleared him without jeopardizing the business, without ruining a twelve-thousand dollar dog. You know?"

Molly, listening, now looks stricken, as if she's lost her best friend. I whine softly and she whirls towards me. "Shh."

Annie doesn't answer right away. "I think," she says at last, "that Molly's lucky to have you as a dad. Whether you're right or wrong about the scent confusion. I'm not at all sure that's what's going on, and even if it is, Doodle isn't ruined. Wouldn't take long to refocus him in training."

Ruined? I'm not following this conversation at all.

"Doesn't matter. Without enough new customers in the next few months, I'll be ruined," the boss says in a grim voice.

No one speaks for a moment. Then, the boss clears his throat. "Sorry to dump that on you. I really appreciate your coming today. And the pudding was great—sorry I wasn't able to eat much."

Annie says, "Completely understandable. I may be crying on your shoulder tomorrow."

A car door opens. "Come on, Chloe, jump in. *Good* girl." The car door shuts and I hear the whine of the window going down. "Josh, don't give up on Doodle yet. He's smart, and, frankly, I'd trust his nose over any results that involved Sid."

Couldn't have said it better myself.

The car vrooms to a start, but Molly doesn't move even after the sound of the wheels and footsteps on gravel have faded and we're left in silence. Instead she stares, at the barn door. Oh no. Tears have pooled in her eyes.

I think I've mentioned that I'm not the touchy-feely sort that so stereotypes humans' images of dogs. Do the work, get paid has been my motto from the get-go. But Molly…

I lick her hand until she bends over to touch me, then lick the tears from off her cheeks, tasting their saltiness.

"Oh, Doodle." She kneels down on the straw, and buries her face into my fur. I stand strong on all four legs and support her weight as she cries, her tears hot against my skin. Finally, she gives a last convulsive shudder, and releases me.

"Oh, Doodle. What are we going to do now?"

Chapter 19

Getting Back Up

HERE'S THE THING I LIKE ABOUT MOLLY. WELL, ONE of the things I like about her. She's a fighter. She's like a scrappy terrier who bounces off the ground after getting a vicious kick, jumps right back up, shakes it off, and comes back for more.

Not that I think terriers are necessarily wise when they behave like this, often threatening a much larger dog or a human with a big boot. And, to be honest, sometimes I worry because Molly doesn't always do the smart thing. But the point is that she's not one to just mope around and do nothing.

So, when she's finished crying, she straightens up and wipes her face with the bottom of her shirt. "I don't believe it," she says. "I'm with Miguel. I just don't believe it."

I'm not sure what she means, but it's always good to be with Miguel. She leads me back into the house and goes straight for the computer. I lie by her feet in case she needs me again, although I can tell by the set of her spine and the angle of her head that she's feeling better. She sits watching that blue screen until the boss tells her it's time for bed.

"I'll take Doodle out," she offers, seeing the boss pick up my leash. She pulls on her jacket, grabs the leash, and soon we're outside in the crisp night air, the single tall streetlight over by the barn casting long shadows as we walk.

Molly has her phone open before we reach the weeds. "Tanya?"

Tanya's voice comes through clearly. "Hey, how'd Doodle do today?"

"Um, not good." Molly explains about the trial while I decide which bush to grace with my mark. Can't decide so I pick a couple of them. No one—no dog that is—will miss the fact that I've been here.

"Somehow, Sid's rigging it," she finishes right about the same time I'm finished. "I'm not sure how, but he threw a major fit when he saw that I had a camera. So he's got to be hiding something. Anyway, you know how Kenny said if I needed anything just ask? Well, I wonder if there's any way that you guys can come down tomorrow before Chloe's trial. Because I think there's some kind of trick and I need help. I hate to ask 'cause it's really early. But it's really important."

Ah—one more spot. I squeeze out a few last drops while Tanya goes off to ask. We're on our way back toward the house when Tanya's voice squawks in the phone. "Yeah, we can do it. Derrin's going to borrow the car and drive us."

"Oh! That's terrific." Molly gives a huge sigh of relief and gives detailed instructions as to how to get to Sid's place. "Can you be there at 8? We won't be there until about 8:30, but if you could get the camera set up—"

I don't hear the rest because I catch the scent of a possum. Hate those things, with their beady little eyes and pointy noses.

I sniff deeply. The scent is faint, so the possum isn't very close. Still. I give a few deep-throated barks. Best to let it know it's not welcome.

"Doodle, hush!" Molly says. "Oh—one more thing. Make sure your cell is charged because we might need to take photos with it, although the pictures won't be as good as with my camera. But we might need it. Also, is there any way you could borrow your mom's video camera? The one she had set up for career day? We need something that can run a long time without shutting off."

"I could ask Mama," Tanya says. "If I say it's for Doodle, she'll say okay. Specially if Kenny's with me."

"Good. Bring the extra battery. Oh, and an extra memory card. But don't let Sid see it. Maybe if we video Chloe's trial and the one before it, we can see what he's trying to hide."

They talk some more while I sniff the air, alert to anything else that might be lurking in the dark, but smell nothing unusual. Even the possum scent has faded. And then the door fills with yellow light and the boss sticks his head out.

"Isn't Doodle done yet? It's late."

"Gotta go," Molly whispers, and shoves the phone in her pocket. "Just finished," she calls to her father.

Soon, we're all in bed in Miguel's spare bedroom—me on my mat by Molly's air mattress, and the boss on the bed, which creaks every time he moves. I go to sleep right away as I always do, but wake up when I feel Molly step on my mat. The boss's soft snores rise and fall in a steady pattern. Molly eases open the bedroom door.

I jump up and squeeze through it before she has a chance to shut me out. Where are we going? To some disappointment, I see that it's only as far as the computer.

Oh, well. One good thing about being a dog is that I can pretty much sleep anywhere and anytime. Not so with humans, based on my own observation, not to mention all those ads on TV for sleeping pills.

So I drift off again. I awake when the computer screen goes black. Molly pads softly towards the bedroom.

"Who watches the watchers?" she whispers to me.

Huh? The boss likes to use that expression, but I never know what he means by it, just as I don't have a clue what Molly's talking about now.

But by the smile that flits across her face, I'm thinking it's something good. And even better, she's finally going back to bed and we can all get a good night's sleep.

Chapter 20

Nabbed at the NABBS

THE BOSS SHUTS OFF THE ENGINE AND LEANS FORWARD, peering towards the big double doors of Sid's barn. "Lots of people here for this time of the morning." He doesn't sound happy, but he's been in a bad mood ever since we got up. And then, with astonishment, "There's Tanya! And Kenny! By the entrance."

Really? I don't smell them. I tilt my head and see them waving at us as a couple of men with leashed dogs file past them.

"Doodle!" the boss admonishes.

Oh. Sorry. But who wouldn't bark a greeting to the Franklins?

Molly waves back. "They came to hang out. That okay?" She's out her door before the boss answers, sliding open the side door.

"Can I take Doodle? They always want to see him."

The boss frowns. "I didn't bring his pinch collar."

"He won't run away," Molly says with confidence. "Not with all that's going on here."

"Okay," the boss says after some hesitation. "I'll go see if I can find Annie." He looks at his watch. "You got your phone?" At Molly's nod, he says, "Her trial's at nine."

"Hey, Dude!" Kenny calls out as Molly and I come up to him and Tanya. Good to see that wide grin on his face.

"Where's Derrin?" Molly asks.

"Mama needed a ride to work," Tanya says, "so he had to go back. He'll come get us when we call."

"That's a lot of gas," Molly says, her brow creasing.

Kenny strokes me under my chin in my favorite spot. I lift my head to help out. "Hey, I'll pay for the gas, any time for The Dude, here. My man's worth it."

"Can't believe he didn't pass," Tanya says.

"Me neither." Molly's voice is grim. "Did you—?"

Tanya nods. "Got here early with Mama's camera. We watched the first dog do the test, and left things set up, just as you said." She bends around Kenny to scratch behind my ear. I could get used to all this attention. I wag my tail in appreciation.

After a furtive glance around, Molly pulls her camera from her pocket and hands it to Kenny. "Can you sneak this in?"

Kenny's big hand folds over it and he slips it in his pocket. "No problem."

Molly says, "I'll get it after the—" but I don't hear the rest as a Jack Russell with an evident grudge against the world, flings himself against the end of his leash in a barking frenzy at a passing Labrador retriever. Fortunately, the Labrador just gives him a "don't be an idiot" stare and moves sedately past.

And then Molly's tugging on the leash and we're moving toward the doors. Hey, what about Tanya and Kenny? They stay behind. In fact, they seem to be wandering off toward the portable toilets, which, frankly, is an area I'd like to sniff out. Molly gives the leash a little jerk. "Come on, Doodle. Don't worry about them." Reluctantly, I take my place by her side.

We're just through the doors, when I catch Sid's unmistakable odor. Or should I say stench?

"Molly," he says, his face frozen into a smile like those mannequins in store windows.

Without a word, Molly pats the pockets of her jacket flat.

"Good girl." Sid almost sounds like he's going to toss her a treat, but Molly keeps walking.

"That's why we split up," she whispers to me. "He doesn't know them, but if they were with me…"

Still not exactly clear as to what she's talking about, but it doesn't matter. Molly waves to the boss and Annie who stands off to the side over by the testing area. We take a place in line in front of the door to the seating area.

And then the doors open to the testing area and Moustache Man comes out, followed by the skinny guard. And then, at our end, the linebacker guard unlocks the door to the viewing room.

We follow a small group of people inside, where we find three rows of bleachers. I know about bleachers from going to different schools in my service-dog training days. Great place to find chips and bits of hot dogs underneath where the people sit, although it never did any good as the trainer would always insist we "leave it." Never been fond of that command. Anyway, there's no smell of hot dogs here, not to mention these bleachers are way too short to fit under.

Some people have already left coats and coolers on the seats. Molly finds a vacant spot on the first bench. After a few minutes, Kenny and Tanya come in but they don't sit with us. In fact, they don't even sit by each other. Kenny goes up to the third bleacher beside a jacket—hey, that's *his* jacket. He sits beside it and pulls it on his lap, looking around nervously. For some reason, Tanya doesn't go with him, but sits on the second row by herself. I wag my tail at both of them, but neither one even looks in our direction.

Then the boss comes rushing in and slides onto the bench beside Molly. "Aren't you going to sit with the Franklins?"

"I'm good here," Molly answers.

The boss frowns. "How come they're not together?"

My question exactly.

Molly shrugs. The boss gives her a sharp look, but says nothing.

Pretty soon, Chloe comes on the screen. It's a little hard for me to watch because of the flickering, which I gather that humans don't see, at least that's what my service dog trainer used to say. But I watch Chloe give an alert. While I've been trained to sit and point with my nose for my alerts, Chloe jumps up and paws at the area. She gets a treat. I watch some more but after a bit, my eyes tire from the flickering screen. So, I lie down and doze off until Chloe's done and we're all getting up to leave.

As we're going out the door, Tanya comes up to Molly. "Here," she whispers, and slips Molly's camera back into Molly's jacket.

I nose Tanya hoping to get an ear scratch but for some reason she ignores me. And once we're through the doors, Kenny and Tanya head off in a different direction. I don't understand what's going on at all.

We hurry over to Annie and Chloe who stand with the judge just inside the doors of the testing area.

"—got every live find but failed on two distractors—" Moustache Man is saying. He has several vials of live bed bugs in his hand, and, as he speaks, bends down picks up another from under a pillow on the bed.

Annie's face sags. "Can you show me where?"

The skinny guard walks past us, peers briefly at Annie and the judge, and takes a position off to the side. I raise my nose in his direction. Interesting…

Molly, watching me, her eyes intent, whispers, "I thought so." Whoa. Tension pours from her, and I can feel her hand trembling through the leash.

"Sure." Moustache Man leads Annie to the nightstand by the bed in the bedroom. He points to the cell phone case that sits by the lamp with oversized shade. Then he leads her to the room with the crib and points to the small stuffed bear.

"That's exactly where Doodle alerted," Molly says in sudden loud voice. "Both places. Isn't that a coincidence? That two dogs would fail on the exactly the same places?"

The boss stares at her. Moustache Man gives Molly a sympathetic smile. "Well, not really. We have several objects we use as distractors that we cycle in and out. So different dogs can fail on the same objects."

But Molly tugs the leash. "Doodle. Find!"

Now? I take a few steps toward the testing area, but Molly gives a gentle tug on the leash and looks the other direction. "Find," she repeats.

So, not in there. Out here. Ah. She must have smelled it, also. I have to say that surprises me, because humans can't smell their way into a garbage bag. But I'm game. I go over to the skinny guard and give the alert.

"I thought so," Molly says, this time out loud, her voice stringy with tension.

"Hey, what's he doin'?" The skinny guard steps back.

I move closer and give the alert again.

"What's going on?" The boss comes up beside Molly.

"What's he doin'?" the skinny guard repeats.

"You have bed bugs on you. Live ones," Molly says, her voice still loud.

The skinny guard takes another step back, but now Annie and Chloe come hurrying over. Annie regards him with narrowed eyes. "Find!" she commands. Chloe starts to circle, takes a few sniffs, moves straight to the guard. She jumps forward, pawing at him.

"Hey, get off!" the skinny guard shouts. He kicks at Chloe, misses, and teeters forward. Something flies out of his windbreaker pocket and bounces on the floor.

"Well, look at that," Annie says. "A phone case. Just like the one on the dresser that both Doodle and Chloe alerted on."

Molly says, "Do you have a small stuffed bear in that pocket also?"

The guard touches his pocket, then jerks his hand away, a guilty expression on his face.

Now the two evaluators join us. "What's this?" Moustache Man points at the phone case lying on the floor.

I catch a motion out of the corner of my eye. Suddenly alert, I turn to see—why it's Sid. He strides towards us, then abruptly stops, stares for a second, then turns and runs toward the back of the building. Very bizarre behavior.

"Doodle," Molly says, and I realize I'm growling. But she looks towards Sid just as he unlocks a door along the back wall and disappears through it.

"What's he up to?"

Can't help wondering that myself. I strain forward until the leash tightens.

"Good idea," Molly says, and together we take off for the door.

"Molly!" a voice cries out—it's Kenny. But Molly doesn't seem to hear. We run to the door. But when we get to it, Molly hesitates. She pulls her camera from her pocket, turns it on, and then eases the handle of the door open. I squeeze my head through, trying to see.

Sid stands behind a folding table in a storeroom, lined at one end with boxes and at the other with a long rack full of tools. The table holds stuffed bears and phone cases that look identical to the ones in the trial, and Sid's tossing them into a backpack.

Molly clicks her camera. He jerks his head up and cries out in alarm.

But what do I smell? I mean other than the distinct and awful Sid cologne? Bed bugs? I shove through the door to get closer. Oops. Didn't mean to push Molly. She stumbles and falls forward inside. The door swings shut behind us.

"You!" The word, low and guttural, carries such menace that my hackles raise and I growl a warning. "You're just always in the wrong place at the wrong time."

Without warning, he lunges forward. "Give me that camera, you little—"

I let loose with a volley of my loudest, most danger-alerting barks. Sid swears, and pushes past Molly, flipping the lock on the door.

Then he grabs her arm. "Give it to me," he grunts.

Molly twists, but can't get free. "Ow!" And then, in the loudest I've ever heard her voice, "Help! Help!"

"Shut-UP!" His arm flies back and then hurtles toward Molly's face, fist closed. I don't think so. I leap at it, grabbing him above the wrist. The arm keeps moving, but the force of my weight deflects it. Sid yelps in pain, and knees me in the ribs before we all crash to the floor. Dazed, I struggle to my feet, but Sid side-arms me in the head. I reel backward. He wrenches the camera from Molly, grabs the backpack, runs to the door that leads outside, and flings it open.

"My camera," Molly cries out, just as a volley of pounding and shouts erupt from behind the locked door.

Sid, now outside, bursts into a run.

I chase after him, my legs spurred by the memory of his fist aiming for Molly's face. I catch up to him just before he gets to a gleaming white oversized pickup.

I leap through the air in a way I've seen done on TV but never attempted before, hoping my weight will bring him crashing to the ground. Instead, I end up with a mouthful of his jacket as I roll off his back.

He stumbles, then plunges forward towards the truck.

I leap again, this time going for his leg. I get another mouthful of clothing but at least it slows him down. He kicks wildly, trying to shake me off, and I almost lose my grip.

From behind, I hear a chorus of shouts. I release the pants and thrust forward, this time sinking my teeth through Sid's jeans and into flesh. He screams. I simultaneously catch Kenny's scent and see him flying through the air like a lineman playing football. He smashes into Sid, who collapses underneath him.

Now all sorts of people come running up, all sorts of voices yelling. Over them all, I hear the boss's, thick with fear, "Molly, are you hurt?", and then I hear her answer, "I'm okay," and then, a few moments later, "Doodle! Off!"

I release my hold on Sid. Kenny's got a good grip on him anyway.

Frankly, I'm panting too hard to pay attention to all the chaos that follows. Not to mention my side throbs from Sid's knee and my head hurts from Sid's fist. Although not as much as I think he hurts from my teeth. Because, in all the accusations flying back and forth between Sid and Molly as to who did what, Sid holds up his arm and then pulls up his pant leg several times to show the bite marks on his skin.

And, at the end, when everyone is finally clearing off, Sid growls, in a voice as lethal as a Rottweiler's bark, "That dog's a menace. Totally vicious. I'll see that he's put down."

Which might have been more frightening if, at the very same time, Pete the Moustache Man wasn't leading him away in handcuffs.

Chapter 21

Zeke's

HAVE I EVER MENTIONED THAT I LOVE ZEKE'S? ANY place that allows dogs is my kind of place, especially if it also has burgers. So it's great to be here with all the Franklins and Annie. The boss invited Miguel, too, who said he appreciated the offer but crowds make him itch. Not sure what he means by that. I take flea meds so I don't itch. We're all here to congratulate Molly—and me, and also Tanya and Kenny, as she keeps reminding everyone—for getting Kenny out of jail and Sid into it.

So we're all sitting in the outside area at Zeke's, around a long white metal table eating burgers. Me on the ground, of course, the rest in brightly painted metal chairs. And I'm happy because I don't even have to wait for Molly to sneak me bites since Mr. Franklin ordered two burgers just for me.

"Thanks, Doodle, for clearing Kenny's name," he says, as he breaks the first one into pieces on a paper plate and then sets it on the ground. "You did more than any of those lawyers."

"And cost a lot less," Mrs. Franklin says, fervently.

Everyone laughs at that. "And Molly—don't know what we'd have done if you hadn't risked…" Mr. Franklin's voice catches and he shakes his head. "Hard times," he says at last, his eyes scrunched together as if he's trying to shut out the memory. "You're a brave girl."

Molly sits at the end of the table with me on the ground on one side and Tanya at the other. "Don't forget Tanya and Derrin," she says again. "And Kenny totally paid me back."

Her face glows with happiness, and her hands, when not putting food in her mouth, rest relaxed on her lap. She hasn't twisted a strand of hair all evening. And she's eaten almost all her burger plus an enormous mound of fries, and most of a chocolate shake. "After seeing the way he tackled Sid—I think he ought to do football as well as basketball."

"Wouldn't break my heart," Mr. Franklin admits with a grin.

Mrs. Franklin shakes her head. "I'm not sure my poor heart can take basketball *and* football."

Kenny, sitting next to Tanya, puts down his burger—his third, I can't help but notice. "Couldn't let him get away with all the evidence," he says, looking pleased.

Mrs. Franklin wipes her face, sets down her napkin, and turns to Molly. "Just exactly what did happen? I've heard bits and pieces but never the whole thing. Only that Doodle flunked his test, but something shady was going on."

"Shady as in fraud," the boss says with some heat. "Sid got hired to manage the training operation at Smithfield's. The owner had sunk tons of money into building the facility and wanted to see a good return both in terms of reputation and money coming in. So Sid was under pressure to get results. He decided to nudge things along a bit by ensuring that the teams that took his training passed, and those that didn't failed."

"How'd he do that? Bribe the judge?" Derrin dips an onion

ring into some catsup.

"Not the judge," the boss says, "the security guard." He sighs and murmurs, "Who watches the watchers?"

Still don't know what that means, and from the blank looks from those around the table, I'm not the only one.

"When Sid promoted the cert trials, he liked to emphasize that he only hired evaluators with vast experience using scent detection dogs, people with impeccable records in law enforcement. And he'd talk about how he kept the trial rooms locked in between the tests so there could be no scent contamination. All good and fine. But Sid's security guard opened the room for the judges, and always did a quick 'sweep' when they'd finished. And he—"

The boss tilts a half-eaten fry at Molly. "But you tell it. You're the one who figured it out. I kept saying the results had to be right because there was no way to skew them. But that wasn't good enough for Molly."

Molly blushes a little, and her fingers stray to a strand of hair, but she looks happy nevertheless. "I couldn't believe that Doodle failed—he's always had a great nose—and then, when Gunther passed, it was just like Annie said, just the opposite of what we expected. So I thought it had to be rigged. And it had to be through the judges or the security guard since they were the only ones with access to the rooms. I'd read about pseudo scents when I had to teach Doodle to find pot—" she takes a sip of her root beer and gives me a little pat on the head.

"Soo *what*?" asks Mr. Franklin.

"Pseudo scents," Annie chimes in, spelling the word. "They're training aids that mimic the scent of real things—different drugs, termites, bed bugs. Trainers use them to imprint the dog on a particular scent. But you didn't use pseudo did you? To train Doodle on pot?"

Now Molly's flush deepens and her fingers steal to her hair. "Um, no. I got a small sample from, um, a friend, who wanted to clear Kenny." Tanya darts a glance at Derrin, but Molly keeps her gaze resolutely on the table. "That I gave to the cops as soon as we were done," she says, the words tumbling out quickly.

"And she did a great job training him," Annie says with pride. "Which is why Josh was so worried that Doodle failed because of scent confusion—" She touches the boss lightly on the arm with an apologetic smile. By the silly grin on his face when he looks down on her, he doesn't mind. "Which, simply put, is when a dog isn't sure which scent he's supposed to be searching for."

As if eager to move on, Molly says, "Anyway, I knew about pseudo scents, and the ones I'd seen on the internet were in little vials."

"That cost $60!" Tanya adds. "So, no way we could afford it."

Molly nods. "But after Doodle failed, I searched some more and found out that they make pens—like markers, really—with pseudo scents, including that of live bed bugs. And I read about how easy it would be to get a dog to give a false alert by simply swiping a pseudo pen over some object. It'd leave no mark. No trace, except to a dog, who could smell it. As Doodle did."

She leans down and gives me a scritch between the ears.

"So I figured maybe that's how Sid was fixing the results. But I still couldn't see when. But then, Sid was so paranoid about cameras and photography, I thought that maybe it was something that could be caught on camera. Just like the video did with Gunther, when we saw how he always watched his handler before alerting."

Molly pauses, takes a few more gulps of root beer. "That's where Tanya and Kenny came in. They brought Mrs. Franklin's video camera, and then—" She points at Tanya who beams back at her.

"Then we snuck it in, and Kenny hid it in his jacket and he taped a complete trial. But even better ..." She points at her brother.

Kenny swallows, grinning. "Then I changed the battery and wrapped it in my coats, so it wouldn't be visible to the guard at the door, and left it running, pointed at the TV, for the time that we had to be out of the room between sessions."

"And what'd you find?" Mrs. Franklin asks, leaning forward with interest.

"That the guard—the thin one—stopped in front of the exact same spots where Doodle gave false alerts. His back was to us, but when Molly saw it..."

"I thought it'd be pretty interesting if Chloe gave false alerts at those same spots, also. And she did. And then Doodle kept sniffing at the guard in an interested way, so I gave the search command and he alerted on the guard's coat pocket and then Chloe did and then the cell phone cover fell out."

"Not one of those pseudo things?" asks Derrin.

"No, the pens were in the back room on a table with duplicates of the stuffed bear and phone covers that the judges used as distractors. That's what Sid was trying to get rid of when I snapped a picture of him. And he went berserk."

"He might have been able to talk his way out of it," the boss adds, "if he hadn't panicked and attacked Molly."

A new scent suddenly makes my nostrils twitch. *Miga*? It can't be. I look up to see Cori heading straight for our table. Didn't know she was coming. From the catch in Molly's breath, I gather she didn't either.

The boss rises out of his chair. "Cori. Glad you could make it."

Molly stares open-mouthed at her mother and then gives her father a quizzical look.

"I invited her," the boss says, flushing a little. "Since we're honoring you, and Cori helped with the Thatcher thing, I thought it'd be, um, appropriate." He introduces Cori to the Franklins.

"Of course, I know Barbara," Cori says.

"And this is Annie Harmon," the boss says. If Molly notices how his hand lingers on Annie's arm, she doesn't show it. But one of Cori's eyebrows lifts slightly.

"Pleased to meet you," she says. "You're a trainer right?" As Annie nods, Cori continues. "Sorry, to be late," She gives an apologetic smile, biting her bottom lip just a little. "And like I said on the phone, I can't stay. I'm actually on my way to the station now. Something's come up. As it always does." She rolls her eyes. "But since this is a celebration because of Molly's work—"

"And Doodle's—" Molly adds, for which I'm grateful.

"And Doodle's," Cori repeats with a smile. "I brought you a gift." She holds out a small, slender, box, the cardboard scuffed and worn and carrying on it an intriguing cluster of scents.

Wide-eyed, Molly lifts the lid and sucks in her breath. "It's beautiful," she says, holding up a small gold object on a thin chain. "A butterfly."

"It was your grandmother's," Cori says, relaxing a little. "Her father gave it to her when she was about your age. He always called her his little butterfly. *Mariposa*. I thought you might like it."

"I *love* it." Molly's eyes shine as she studies it. She holds it around her neck.

"Let me help you." Cori bends over and clasps the chain, then straightens up.

"And for the rest of you—I thought you might like to know the detectives in Fairfax County say the case against Sid is looking good. Naturally, Sid swears he didn't do anything wrong and all the evidence is circumstantial, but the cops had enough cause with his attack on Molly to get a search warrant. Guess what they found? The closed-circuit TV from the trials also went into a small set in Sid's office. So he could watch the judges set up the course, text the guard, and manipulate the outcome. If he wanted a team to fail, he'd have the guard substitute a duplicate item for the distractor, one marked with the pseudo live scent. Then it looked like the dog was alerting on the dead bugs, but really it was alerting on live ones."

"So that's how the guard knew," Molly says. "I wondered."

"Well, you figured out most of it. And it turns out that Sid has a record, under an alias, for fraud when working with a termite company down in Florida. Add that to a full confession from the security guard—who, by the way, also has a record—and well, I think there's good reason to be optimistic."

This makes everyone smile and several people start talking at once.

Cori bends over to Molly, and in a much quieter voice, says, "I'm really sorry about … how things went on your visit. Can we try again? Maybe just an afternoon or something until things at work calm down? Maybe next Saturday?"

"That—that'd be *great*." Why Molly's trembling, but not from fear or sadness unless I'm totally incompetent at reading humans, which obviously I'm not. She fingers the butterfly.

"I'll call your dad in a few days and work things out."

Cori's phone buzzes. She silences it. "I really have to go," she says. "But Molly, you should be proud. Two different crooks trying to get away with something and you outsmarted them both."

Molly flushes and smiles, and then leans over to pat me on the head. "Couldn't have done it without Tanya and Kenny," she says. "Or Doodle." She runs a hand down my back.

"I only outsmarted them because Doodle outsniffed them."

Epilogue

"FIND." THE BOSS'S COMMAND COMES IN A FIRM, LOW voice. We're at the Perfect Stay Hotel, standing in the doorway of a hotel suite that's at the top of a very tall building.

I lift my nose and sample the scents. Nothing on the desk, nor the chair with the padded bottom beside it. I go to the couch. Nothing on the back or the fat cushions. But—I sniff some more, sorting the scents—over here, lower, lower . . . Yes! I give the alert to the back bottom corner of the couch.

"Good dog," the boss says, giving me a treat, which tastes mighty good, because once again I haven't had breakfast.

Pete the Moustache Man and Ortega make notes on their clipboards. Beyond the door, in the hall where Molly and Annie wait, I hear Annie's phone buzz, and then the low tones of her voice.

"Find," the boss commands again. So I ignore Annie's voice and get back to work.

I sweep the rest of the room but find no more evidence of bed bugs. In the first bedroom, however, I catch the scent immediately behind a throw cushion on a padded chair. I move closer, sniffing hard.

Hah. Those are dead bugs. Can't fool me. I move on and finish the bedroom, alerting on a corner of a baseboard, and on the bottom of a picture frame over a small desk. More treats, more writing on clipboards.

I thoroughly search the next bedroom but only find a distractor under the pillow on the bed. Naturally, I don't give an alert.

Finally, I check out the bathroom. Don't usually find bed bugs here, but what's this? I move in and test the area around a wicker clothes hamper. Yes, indeed. I give the alert, get my treat, and Pete announces the trial is done.

We go back into the hall. Annie is still on the phone. "Oh, I understand completely," she says in a soothing voice. "You're making the right decision for both of you."

Pete and Ortega put their pens away. They move down the hall for a brief consultation, while the boss and Molly look on with anxious faces.

"Okay," Annie says into her phone. "Two this afternoon." She snaps it shut just as Pete and Ortega walk back, clipboards under their arms.

"Perfect!" Pete says with a broad smile that makes his moustache wave. And in near-record time. He zeroed in on the vials just like that." He snaps a finger.

Now everyone is smiling, and the boss and Molly give each other a high five.

"Did you hear that?" Molly throws her arms around my neck and gives me a big kiss on the nose. "Perfect!!"

"I knew you'd do well," Annie says, giving me a few of her excellent treats as she scratches me under the chin.

Then the boss shakes hands with Pete and Ortega, thanking them again, and we head down the hall to the elevator. The judges stay behind because, according to the boss, they're going to be testing dogs all afternoon.

"Guess who just called," Annie says as we get into the elevator. I brace myself since these thing *move* and they always make my stomach feel a little weird.

She doesn't wait for anyone to guess. "Jerry Alben. And I have good news and even better news."

"Gunther passed the test?" the boss asks in surprise.

"No, he failed it yesterday. The good news is that right after he failed, Jerry called the owner of Smithfield's and demanded his money back for all the training Sid gave him, saying if they didn't repay him, Jerry would sue them for fraud. And the owner, who's already got more bad publicity than he can handle, agreed to the refund. Jerry says he's going to sue the original trainer, too."

"So what happens to Gunther?" Molly asks.

Annie smiles. "That's the better news. Jerry asked me if I'd take him and find him a good home. Jerry's decided not to use a dog in his business."

"Good decision!" Molly says fervently.

Annie and the boss both nod in agreement. "He's going to drop Gunther at Miguel's this afternoon," she adds.

The elevator comes to a stop, and we walk into the lobby just as another dog and handler enter the elevator.

Annie watches as the elevator doors close, then turns to the boss. "So how does it feel to have a genuine certified scent dog?"

"Great!" The boss squats down and scratches under my chin, something he doesn't usually do since we generally keep our relationship more on a business level. "*Good* work, Doodle," he says in a low voice, with such feeling that I can't help but wag my tail.

He pulls out a few extra treats from his pouch and feeds them to me. And then Molly bends over and scratches behind my ears in that way that I love.

"It feels *great,*" he repeats.

Couldn't have said it better myself.

Acknowledgements

A huge thanks to Doug Summers for his generous gift of time and information. In 2005, along with Bill Whistine, Summers helped train one of the very first bed bug detection dogs in the U.S. In addition to entertaining me with a variety of funny and sometimes hair-raising anecdotes from the world of scent-detection dogs and handlers, Summers gave me insight into the day-to-day workings of trainers, as well as into the protocols, issues and controversies surrounding odor recognition tests for bed bug dogs.

Kim La France patiently answered my many questions about training scent detection dogs. Steve Hawkins, president of 5 Star Environments, gave me valuable insight into the real life world of bed bug detection dogs and handlers.

Marti Jones, the Executive Director and Senior Staff Attorney at the Immigration Project in Bloomington, Illinois, kindly gave me another round of interviews that increased my understanding of the history of Mexican immigrants in the United States, with particular insight into the problems of families with "mixed", i.e. legal and illegal, status. She also helped me construct a more realistic background for Molly's mother and aunt.

Any errors, regarding either scent detection dogs or the Mexican-American immigration experience, are, of course, my own, and any wrong-doing in the book is purely from my imagination and not based on any living person or organization.

First readers Sara Hoskinson Frommer and Barbara Farnworth gave me good insights into the early drafts of the book. Copyeditors Lyn Worthen and Ardis Kenney used their eagle eyes to help me clean up a host of errors before submitting the final draft to Laurel Fork Press.

To my son, Joe, another round of heartfelt thanks for his encouragement and for his countless hours of computer and Photoshop support.

Finally, thanks to Shadow, my intrepid, amiable-dominant, extremely independent labradoodle, who upended my expectations of how a "good" dog should behave, and has given me endless material for Doodle's antics. That's a good thing, right?

About the Author

Susan J. Kroupa is a dog lover currently owned by a 70 pound labradoodle whose superpower is bringing home dead possums and raccoons. She is also an award-winning author whose fiction has appeared in *Realms of Fantasy*, and in a variety of professional anthologies, including *Bruce Coville's Shapeshifters*. Her non-fiction publications include features about environmental issues and Hopi Indian culture for *The Arizona Republic, High Country News, American Forests*, and the *Bristol Herald-Courier*.

She now lives in the Blue Ridge Mountains in Southwestern Virginia, where she's busy writing the next Doodlebugged mystery, as well as Doodlewhacked, a blog about the real-life travails of raising a very independent, high-energy labradoodle.

More Molly and Doodle

Bed-Bugged

Doodlebugged Mysteries #1, now available in trade paper and in a variety of ebook formats

Ask Doodle why he flunked out of service dog school and he'll tell you: smart and obedient don't always go hand in hand. Now he has a new job sniffing out bed bugs for his new boss, Josh Hunter. The best part of the job? Molly, the boss's ten-year old daughter, who slips Doodle extra treats when she's not busy snapping photos with her new camera. But Molly has secrets of her own. And when she enlists Doodle's help to solve a crime, his nose and her camera lead them straight to danger. A charming mystery for dog lovers of all ages.

Doodlebugged Mysteries #3

Watch for Molly and Doodle's next adventure, Spring 2013 in trade paper and ebook

More from Susan J. Kroupa

Gabriel & Mr. Death

Now available in a variety of ebook formats

Gabriel is a coon hound with an unusual gift: he can see Mr. Death. He doesn't think too hard on it until one Christmas Eve when Mr. Death comes for the person Gabriel loves most. He can't let that happen, no sir, no way. No matter what a poor hound has to do. A touching story about a dog's love and loyalty and the healing power of family.

Made in the USA
San Bernardino, CA
09 May 2017